*Quinn Gresham wants to meet
with you as soon as possible.*

Kathleen Kerns paced her office, having recovered
from the first moments of paralysis after she had
found her secretary's note. She wanted a cigarette, a
craving that hit only in moments of extreme tension.
She popped a stick of gum into her mouth and
resumed pacing.

As far as Kathleen knew, Quinn had never
contributed to her employer's campaign fund, nor
did he have any other dealings with the congressman.
What possible business could Quinn have with this
office now?

She forced herself to sit at her desk, determined to
dictate some letters, but her glance fell unerringly on
the note containing Quinn's name. Her already
wavering concentration was shattered. Resting her
elbow on the desk, she placed her chin in her hand
and stared unseeingly at the wall before her.

Did the past ever really die?

Dear Reader:

Romance offers us all so much. It makes us "walk on sunshine." It gives us hope. It takes us out of our own lives, encouraging us to reach out to others. Janet Dailey is fond of saying that romance is a state of mind, that it could happen anywhere. Yet nowhere does romance seem to be as good as when it happens *here*.

Starting in February 1986, Silhouette Special Edition is featuring the AMERICAN TRIBUTE—a tribute to America, where romance has never been so wonderful. For six consecutive months, one out of every six Special Editions will be an episode in the AMERICAN TRIBUTE, a portrait of the lives of six women, all from Oklahoma. Look for the first book, *Love's Haunting Refrain* by Ada Steward, as well as stories by other favorites—Jeanne Stephens, Gena Dalton, Elaine Camp and Renee Roszel. You'll know the AMERICAN TRIBUTE by its patriotic stripe under the Silhouette Special Edition border.

AMERICAN TRIBUTE—six women, six stories, starting in February.

AMERICAN TRIBUTE—one of the reasons Silhouette Special Edition is just that—Special.

The Editors at Silhouette Books

JEANNE STEPHENS
A Few Shining Hours

Silhouette Special Edition

Published by Silhouette Books New York

America's Publisher of Contemporary Romance

SILHOUETTE BOOKS
300 East 42nd St., New York, N.Y.   10017

ISBN: 0-373-09308-X

First Silhouette Books printing May 1986

America's Publisher of Contemporary Romance

Printed in the U.S.A.

JEANNE STEPHENS

is an incurable romantic, so a career as a romance novelist is a natural for her. Her own romantic hero is her husband, and he lives in each of her fictional heroes. Like Jeanne, her heroines are one-man women who view marriage as the ultimate romantic experience.

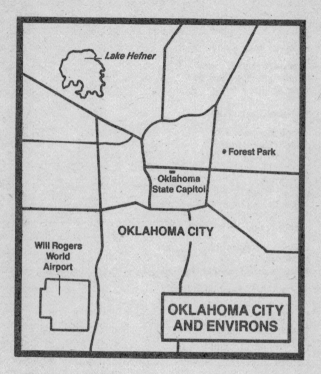

Lake Hefner

• Forest Park

Oklahoma
State Capitol

OKLAHOMA CITY

Will Rogers
World
Airport

**OKLAHOMA CITY
AND ENVIRONS**

Chapter One

Kathleen Kerns paced her office, staring at the toes of her slender black patent pumps. She'd been pacing since recovering from the first moments of paralysis that had been caused by finding her secretary's note buried beneath a pile of messages on her desk.

Quinn Gresham wants to meet with you as soon as possible. You have a free hour tomorrow at four.

She wanted a cigarette. She'd given up smoking seven months ago, and the craving rarely hit her anymore. Quitting hadn't been as difficult as she'd expected; it was only in moments of high anxiety or extreme tension that she wanted the comforting solace of nicotine. She pulled open a desk drawer, took a stick of gum from the pack she always kept there and popped it into her mouth. She resumed her pacing.

A few moments later she jumped as the silence was broken by a staccato clatter in the outer office. Renee had turned on the printer to run off the congressman's letter to a select group of his constituents, those who had made generous contributions to his last campaign for election to the U.S. House of Representatives from Oklahoma's Fifth District.

As far as Kathleen knew, Quinn Gresham had never contributed to the congressman's campaign fund or had any other dealings with him. She was certain he hadn't during the time she had been working for Congressman Smythe. Kathleen wondered what possible business Quinn could have with this office as she forced herself to sit at her desk, determined to dictate some letters before her luncheon meeting. She had trained herself to put on blinders and concentrate on one thing at a time. Compartmentalizing her thoughts was the only way to tackle the work load that awaited her daily without being overwhelmed. As one of Congressman Jefferson Smythe's two top aides, she was in charge of the Oklahoma City office. The other aide, Jeb Drewly, served as her counterpart in Washington.

She turned on her dictating machine. "Letter to Professor Sanders Weinberg, Oklahoma City University...I think he's in the chemistry department. You'll have to check that, Renee.... Dear Professor Weinberg, in regard to your request that Congressman Smythe address the Conference on Environmental Health at O.C.U. on..." She'd forgotten the date and couldn't put her hand on the letter, which had been right there on top of the take-care-of-immediately stack a moment ago. Sighing, she switched off the machine while she searched for the letter.

But her glance fell unerringly on the note containing Quinn's name, and her already wavering concentration was shattered. Resting one elbow on the desk, she placed her chin in her hand and stared, unseeing, at the tan-draped wall before her.

Did the past ever really die?

She had known for some time that Quinn kept a residence in Oklahoma City, but she had filed that information in the compartment with things she didn't want to think about. It had been fifteen years since she'd last seen Quinn, and the possibility of meeting him again after all that time was terrifying.

She wished she could refuse to see him. But what excuse could she give? If he'd called her at home, that would be one thing, but he'd made the request through her secretary. Since he'd phoned the office, he obviously wanted to see her on a business matter, but that didn't make the prospect any more welcome.

Kathleen was employed by Congressman Smythe to be his liaison with his constituency in the state, and Quinn Gresham was a successful member of Oklahoma City's business community. Political reality being what it was, there simply wasn't any way out. She would have to see Quinn sooner or later, and until she knew what he wanted, she was going to worry.

Having extracted all the flavor from her gum, she tossed it into the wastebasket as she left her office.

"Renee, did Mr. Gresham say what he wanted to see me about?"

The middle-aged secretary was applying gummed address labels to envelopes. She looked up and said apologetically, "No, I tried to find out, but he said the matter was complicated and he'd prefer to take it up with you. I phoned his secretary, but she didn't even know he'd asked for an appointment and had no idea what it was about."

If Renee couldn't find out what Quinn wanted, nobody could. The secretary's ten years of working in Congressman Smythe's office had forced her to become adept at ferreting out information. Kathleen frowned in consternation.

"I did a little background checking on Gresham," Renee offered. "He's president of Gresham Enterprises. It's an importing business. They retail quality imports through the Worldwide Treasures stores. There are about fifty of them in the Southwest—two here in town—and the business is in the process of expanding into the North and Northeast. The corporation went public a couple of years ago, and last year gross sales topped thirty million. My broker has the company on his growth-stock buy list. I got a copy of the Value Line sheet on Gresham Enterprises, if you want to see it.''

Kathleen smiled at the last bit of information. Renee's avocation was the stock market. She studied technical and fundamental analyses as eagerly as any gambler ever worked out a system to beat the casinos in Vegas. She put every dollar she could spare into the market, and she was a savvy investor. Kathleen had taken Renee's advice on a stock purchase last year and sold the shares at double her cost ten months later.

"I have a general idea of what he does for a living," Kathleen said. "I just don't know of any business he has with the congressman."

"Maybe it has something to do with import restrictions," Renee said.

"Maybe," Kathleen mused, "but it's frustrating that he—er, people won't give you a hint of what they're after. How am I supposed to prepare for the meeting?"

Renee watched her boss comb her fingers restlessly through her sable hair; she hadn't missed Kathleen's slip of the tongue, either. Kathleen was troubled.

"Well," Kathleen said reluctantly, "call his secretary and see if he can make it at four tomorrow." She started back to her office, but halted in the doorway. "Renee, you wouldn't happen to have a cigarette, would you?"

Renee eyed Kathleen with sympathy. "I haven't carried a pack for two years." A former smoker herself, Renee had given Kathleen a lot of moral support when Kathleen decided to stop. "I could run over to the mall—if you're really sure you want one." Renee paused an instant, then couldn't resist adding, "but you'll hate yourself tomorrow."

Kathleen hesitated for a heartbeat. Then she squared her shoulders in her black-and-white print silk shirt. "Forget I said that. I'll chew another stick of gum."

"Attagirl," Renee said approvingly. She stared at the office door after Kathleen had closed it. Something had really gotten under Kathleen's skin, evidently something to do with Quinn Gresham. Seeing Kathleen in such a state was rare enough to arouse Renee's curiosity, not to mention her concern. Did Kathleen know Quinn Gresham? Her manner indicated that she didn't want to meet with him. It took a lot to disturb the air of imperturbability that her attractive boss wore like a cloak. What *did* Quinn Gresham want? Judging from Kathleen's reaction, it probably had to do with something more upsetting than import restrictions.

A brief afternoon shower had cooled the air. It soaked the thirsty plain of central Oklahoma before it moved on to the east, washing the tender green grass and fragile early flowers. The day was rich with April fertility as spring burst forth in fleeting celebration before the long scorching summer crushed it. The late afternoon sunshine filtered through thin clouds in streams of slanting light that quickly dried the puddles in the street.

With a sigh of the first contentment she'd known all day, Kathleen steered her sporty little sedan toward her home in northeast Oklahoma City. Sometimes it took almost an hour to make the drive from her office near the state capitol complex during the rush hour. The city was one of the largest in the country in terms of square miles. With no natural barriers to stop it, it sprawled across the prairie like oil spilling from a gushing well.

She drove with the car windows down. The air still smelled of rain, and the breeze tossed the shining strands of her hair across her face. She pushed at them idly as she darted around the car ahead of her, then shot deftly into a gap in the outside lane, anticipating her exit.

During the afternoon she'd convinced herself that she would deal with Quinn when the time came and not try to anticipate what he wanted. Probably it was something innocuous, perhaps some strings he wanted Congressman Smythe to pull for him in Washington. Conjuring up dire improbabilities would serve no purpose except to make her a nervous wreck.

Leaving the freeway, Kathleen entered the quiet residential neighborhood where she lived. She admired her neighbors' yards as she passed. Most of the people on her block did their own mowing and gardening and took pride in their handiwork. Kathleen's was the only two-family dwelling on a street of single-family homes. She leased the other half of the brick duplex she'd purchased a year ago to a fifty-six-year-old widow, Maggie Owens. Kathleen was sorry that Maggie was visiting her daughter in Topeka at the moment; she would have liked having someone to chat with. She and Maggie occasionally shared an evening meal, and Kathleen definitely would have suggested it today if Maggie had been home.

As she let herself into her side of the duplex, she hummed a tune to dispel the silence. She tossed her purse on the glass-topped breakfast table, then went through the compact well-equipped kitchen and into the large living-dining area with its beamed cathedral ceiling and celery-colored carpeting. After moving to the atrium doors that overlooked the flagstone patio, she drew the draperies open wide.

Kathleen had spent hours planting and cultivating the lawn surrounding the patio. Trees and beds of shubbery were outlined with railroad ties. In the center, stretching from the edge of the patio to the tall cedar fence that marked the back boundary of the lot, she had created a rock garden, carefully planned so that it sported blooms of one variety or another from March until the first winter frost.

At present clumps of tulips and daffodils lavished splashes of red, pink and yellow about the garden. Kathleen stood there and drank in the beauty. These early days of April were, she thought, the loveliest in the garden. Perhaps because the first blossoms were so welcome after the long, dreary winter—even more appreciated because their beauty was fleeting. A week, two at the most, and the blossoms would begin to lose color, then droop and finally drop away. Yet those brief days were worth all the planting and weeding and watering that the flowers required to be born in such glory, grace the landscape for a few shining hours and then die until another spring.

A few shining hours...

Kathleen was unprepared for the sudden, hot tears that misted her vision, and she turned away from the garden in dismay. She had been a fool to believe she could get through this evening without thinking about Quinn and the past.

During their school days in a small town that became an Oklahoma City suburb when the city grew out to meet it, Quinn, with his sandy hair and laughing blue eyes, had been her brother Patrick's best friend. Quinn's divorced mother, a nurse, had worked the hospital night shift, slept days and often worked overtime on weekends because they needed the money so urgently. She had little time or energy left to give to her son. Consequently Quinn spent more time at the Kernses' house than he did at his own home.

Patrick and Quinn, four years older than Kathleen, had teased her unmercifully, let her tag along with them occasionally and had a code of conduct for her boyfriends that was stricter than her parents'. When Patrick and Quinn went away to college, Kathleen said she would be glad to be rid of their overzealous protection, but she had missed them terribly.

Eventually she realized that she had been in love with Quinn for as long as she could remember. His phone call on her seventeenth birthday meant more to her than the presents from her family or the white orchid her high school boyfriend had pinned to her dress later that year on the night of her first prom.

Her first and last prom, as it turned out, but missing the senior prom hadn't even been a minor disappointment after the heartache of the months that preceded it.

She'd turned seventeen in the April of her junior year in high school. Patrick and Quinn were coming home for spring break, and Kathleen had felt as though her feet wouldn't touch the ground. She didn't think it was possible to be any happier than she was that spring as she waited impatiently to see Quinn for the first time since Christmas vacation. In addition to the phone call on her birthday, he had written her twice during the spring semester and responded to her hints about the girls he was romancing with, "No, Kath, all the women on campus aren't following me around, begging me to take them out. Impossible to believe, I know, but it's true. In fact, I haven't seen one around here who can hold a candle to you."

He'd been teasing her, of course, but she'd memorized those words and repeated them to herself endlessly.

Quinn came to the Kernses' house for dinner the first evening of that week. Before he arrived Kathleen changed clothes five times and rearranged her hair twice. But it was worth the extra effort when she walked into the living room and was greeted by Quinn's bear hug and delighted whoop. "Patrick, would you look at this! We turn our backs for a few months and Kath's all grown up."

He'd held her away from him and looked down at her with laughter in his blue eyes. He was so dear he had taken her breath away.

It was during dinner that Quinn dropped his bomb. "Hey, everybody, did Patrick tell you I'm quitting school to be a helicopter pilot?"

His announcement was met with stunned silence. Finally Kathleen's father, who had suffered a heart attack that January and was recuperating slowly, uttered the protest that was in all their minds. "But, Quinn, another year and you'll have your degree."

Quinn shrugged that off. "Mom can't afford to help me any longer. The last three years have about bankrupted her. Besides, I don't know what I want to do for the rest of my life. Maybe I'll have a better idea when I come back from Nam."

If you come back. The thought had flashed into Kathleen's mind from out of nowhere.

"I'm leaving Saturday," Quinn went on.

To Kathleen at that time, Vietnam had been just a place somewhere on the other side of the world where Americans were getting wounded and killed in an unpopular war. The story of the My Lai massacre had come out the previous year and shocked the nation. Antiwar demonstrations were increasing and there had been an article in the newspaper about young Americans moving to Canada to evade the draft. She didn't want Quinn going to Vietnam, perhaps dying for no good reason. The thought brought a lump to her throat, and she couldn't speak.

"Kath," Patrick said, "we're having a going-away party for Quinn Friday night at the lake. You're invited."

Quinn winked at her. "And you better be there."

There was a time when Kathleen had dwelt endlessly on how different her life would have been if she hadn't gone to the party. But Quinn had said he wanted her there, and wild horses couldn't have prevented her.

The party was held in a summer cottage that belonged to somebody's parents who had stayed in town for the weekend. By the time Kathleen and Patrick arrived the party was in full swing. Rock music shook the rafters, and inhibitions were being drowned in beer.

"This," said Patrick, surveying the crowd, "could get out of hand. Maybe I shouldn't have brought you, sis."

"Don't worry," Kathleen told him, as she scanned the room for a sight of Quinn. "I can take care of myself." It was difficult to identify anybody in the dimly lighted room crammed with dancing couples.

Patrick got her a cola. "I promised Mom I'd keep an eye on you, so lay off the beer."

Kathleen grimaced. "Gladly. I hate the stuff."

Quinn spotted them and came over. He had obviously consumed quite a lot of beer already. Swaying slightly, he clapped Patrick on the shoulder. "Some bash, huh?" He had to yell to be heard above the din.

Patrick frowned. "You better take it easy, buddy. You wouldn't want to pass out at your own party."

"What are you? My conscience?" Quinn asked with a grin. "Do me a favor and don't hassle me, Patrick. How often does a guy get a send-off like this? I have to make the most of it. I sure won't be going to any more parties for a while."

Kathleen had never known Quinn to drink too much before. She wondered if he was trying to blot out thoughts of what awaited him in Vietnam. Maybe he regretted the step he was taking, now that it was too late to change his mind.

"Dance with me, Kath?"

"Sure, Quinn."

After that the night had taken on the hazy quality of a dream. The deep throbbing of the music joined with the beat of Kathleen's heart until she couldn't separate one from the other. She moved in and out of Quinn's arms, laughing, her hair and full skirt swirling around her until exhaustion overcame her.

"I have to sit the next one out," she'd panted.

"It's too hot in here anyway," Quinn had said. "Let's go for a walk." He had downed several more beers between dances, and Kathleen thought it would be an excellent idea for him to get some fresh air.

They walked around the lake, Quinn unsteadily until Kathleen put her arm around his waist and he threw his arm over her shoulders.

His high spirits evaporated as they walked, and he grew silent, as though he didn't have to pretend with her.

"Quite a party," Kathleen commented finally.

"Yeah."

"You have a lot of friends, Quinn."

"Yeah," he said again, and then, "I don't want to go back yet. Let's sit down." He dropped to the high grassy bank that overlooked the lake and pulled her down beside him. Holding her hand in his, he looked at it in the moonlight. Pensively he traced the veins on the back of her hand with his finger. After a long moment he glanced at her and said gravely, "You're beautiful tonight, Kath. Did I tell you that?"

She shook her head, grateful for the darkness, because a tear was sliding down her cheek.

"I'll bet you have more boyfriends than you know what to do with."

"Not really," she said, her throat aching. She couldn't tell him that every boy she knew suffered by comparison with him.

"I don't believe it. They'd have to be blind."

"Maybe that's it." She tried for a smile.

"You really don't have a steady?"

"No. There isn't anybody I want to spend that much time with."

"Good," he said, and she wondered why it mattered to him. He lifted his hand to trace the line of her cheek and jaw. "You take your time, honey."

His gentle, wondering touch undid her. She threw her arms around him and sobbed, "Oh, Quinn, I'm going to miss you so much!"

His arms tightened around her with convulsive strength. She could hardly breathe. His cheek pressed against hers, and he buried his face in her hair. "Kath...Kath," he muttered brokenly.

Then he was kissing her, and the dam that had held her years of love for Quinn in check broke. She was overwhelmed by the bittersweet flood.

It didn't occur to her to be afraid. She had known Quinn all her life; even drunk, he would never hurt her. Nothing about that night was real, anyway. It was all a dream.

He wrenched his mouth from hers and groaned, "I shouldn't be doing this."

Kathleen's lips traced his jawline, hungry for the taste of him. She had fantasized about this moment forever, it seemed. "If you stop now," she whispered as she drew him closer, "I'll never forgive you." The last word was muffled as their mouths found each other again.

The kiss was poignant, drugging. Kathleen thought dimly that she'd never realized before how intoxicating a kiss could be. Each kiss grew deeper and hungrier.

Without knowing when it had happened, Kathleen realized that they were prone in the grass, their bodies fused together. She tangled her fingers in his hair, needing to bring him closer still, even though her body was already molded to his as if it had been created for no other purpose. She could feel his heart pounding with the same churning rhythm as her own. Unnoticed, her blouse came open under his hand, and they began to explore each other.

She couldn't remember a time when she hadn't known Quinn. She had known him as well as anyone could know a friend, yet never like this. The newness of it mesmerized her.

Quinn's lips found the smooth skin of her throat, lingering and savoring the sweetness before moving on to find her closed eyelids and seal them with the whisper of a kiss.

She discovered that the dark angle where his jaw met his neck tasted musky and masculine. She was learning things about him that she had only imagined before, and she thought it might take the rest of her life to learn everything she wanted to know. The ridge of his collarbone was prominent and hard. She traced it with her tongue. The hollow at the base of his throat was dark and deep. She tasted that, too. She had barely started her intoxicating investigation of him when his mouth demanded that hers return to it.

The kiss pierced her with its power and left her giddy. With a moan of surrender she spread her hands against his back and crushed him to her. Quinn plundered her sweet mouth, laying claim to her very breath. She was limp and defenseless in his arms.

When his lips parted from hers, she murmured a soft protest. Quinn lifted his head only enough to allow the moonlight to fall on her face. Her eyes were dark and heavy, her mouth soft and swollen from his kisses.

"I'm drunk," he said roughly, "but I don't know if it's from the beer or you."

She smiled dreamily. "I'm drunk, too, and I haven't had any beer."

His grip on her tightened, and he lowered his head until his warm breath against her ear made her shiver. "I have no right to want you . . . but I do."

"You have more right than anyone," she murmured as the need in him compelled his mouth to find hers again.

Kathleen felt the world teeter away. Self-denial forgotten, he provided no further opportunity for her to change her mind. She would not have taken it if he had.

His hands moved over her with a heightened urgency. His mouth trailed down her throat, hungry and demanding. His hands freed her body of the restraints of her clothing, then his mouth traveled to her breast. Kathleen gasped with surprised pleasure. She knew the ache of desire for the first time in her seventeen years as his hands and mouth aroused and ravished her.

She moved restlessly under him as her womanly instincts stirred. It felt so right, she thought wonderingly, so natural.

There, beneath the stars, with the moon a silver globe shimmering on the surface of the lake, Quinn taught her the wild and reckless abandon of young love.

Nothing had prepared Kathleen for the intensity of it. Her world narrowed to include only the tingling of her flesh under his hands, the hard, rippling muscles of his body, the moist bliss of his kisses. The stars overhead, the dark, glittering lake and the grassy bank upon which they lay infused those moments with a reality that was timeless and primitive.

Afterward, while she was still wrapped tightly in his arms, with the smells of spring and Quinn so intermingled that she didn't know which was which, she told him that she wasn't sorry it had happened. How could she regret anything as beautiful as what they had shared?

Later she learned that that night had marked the end of her childhood in more ways than one. Her naive assurances to Quinn had been nonsense, but she hadn't known it then. At that moment she couldn't even have imagined the pain that would come from those few shining hours on Quinn's last night at home.

Like the gardener who works and toils to enjoy two weeks of spring blossoms, she would wonder many times in the years that followed whether those few hours had been worth the terrible cost. With the benefit of hindsight, would she do the same thing?

Eventually there was no doubt in her mind about the answer. There was nothing in the world for which she would willingly pay that price again.

Chapter Two

Kathleen reached for a jelly bean from the dish on her desk. If I keep eating these things, she thought morosely, I'll get fat. But if I don't eat them, I'm going to break down and smoke a cigarette. Which is worse, she wondered, excess pounds or damaged lungs? Bad lungs, she decided, reaching for another jelly bean. Once her four o'clock meeting was over she would be able to dispense with the candy, anyway.

She glanced at her watch. Nine minutes till four, one minute later than the last time she'd looked. How many jelly beans could a person eat in nine minutes? She sucked on the piece of candy to make it last.

Disgusted with her lack of willpower, she grabbed the dish and put it out of sight in a desk drawer. She went to the door and said, "Renee, would you make fresh coffee before Mr. Gresham arrives?"

The secretary looked up from *The Wall Street Journal.* "Sure thing." Kathleen closed the door, and Renee went to brew the coffee, wondering how well her boss had slept the night before. Kathleen had been obviously tense all day.

At four o'clock sharp Kathleen heard Renee speaking in the outer office. "I'll tell her you're here, Mr. Gresham."

"Thank you."

Quinn. Even if Renee hadn't called him by name, she would have recognized the deep voice. Instantly she dropped the report she had been reading, and her hands clenched into tight fists. Panic clutched her throat. Kathleen forced herself to take deep, calming breaths. Stupid and pointless, she thought as she spread her fingers on the desk top. Resentments shouldn't survive for fifteen years.

Her telephone buzzed. She cleared her throat and depressed one of the buttons on the telephone's base. "Yes?"

"Mr. Gresham to see you," Renee announced.

"Ask him to come in." In the moment before he entered her office, Kathleen debated whether she should receive him seated or standing. Standing, she would have to shake his hand, and that would require a proximity that she didn't want; he might even feel an embrace, for old times' sake, was expected of him. It would be awkward for both of them. She would remain seated at her desk, she decided.

She smoothed her hair as she heard the door opening, and arranged her face in a bland welcome.

A fraction shy of six feet, he looked taller in his gray businessman's suit. The illusion was caused by his leanness, she thought in the moment before his blue eyes found her brown ones.

"Hello, Kathleen. It's good to see you again." The white of his teeth was exaggerated by a deep tan.

"Quinn. You're looking well," she said with a slight smile. Through her nervousness, Kathleen noted that he was more attractive than ever. Fifteen years had added a hairline scar along one cheek and creases to his rawboned face, which managed to be arresting without being classically handsome. Masculine was the appropriate word to describe Quinn Gresham. His hair was the same sandy blond she remembered, curling over the tops of his ears and the back of his white collar. His thick, light-colored brows were slightly arched over eyes that studied her with the acute concentration she had almost forgotten. Success in business had given him an ease of manner that, Kathleen knew, covered a shrewd mind. At thirty-six he was one of the state's leading young entrepreneurs. She had heard it said that Quinn Gresham had the touch of a Midas and the drive of an Alexander. She watched as his mouth formed the lopsided smile that had once made her heart flip over and now made her want to flee.

"You too," he said.

Her impersonal tone and the fact that she had not stepped around the desk to greet him stifled any impulse he had to touch her. Instead he let his eyes run over her white silk shirt and green linen jacket, skim the shining hair that curved under at her earlobes and return to her face. "Fifteen years has changed you."

"It's a long time," she retorted, angry that she wanted to know whether he considered the changes for better or worse. For an instant she felt like a silly, gangling adolescent again. "Everything has changed."

"It sure has." He glanced around the large office as his teeth flashed in a grin. Apparently the fact that she ran Congressman Smythe's state office was difficult for him to assimilate. "Fifteen years ago I'd have bet you'd be long married by now, running a house in the suburbs and chasing after three or four kids. Evidently I didn't know you as well as I thought."

"Evidently." She met his perplexed look coolly. She inclined her head toward the armchair that faced her across the broad expanse of the desk. "Wouldn't you like to sit? I'll ask my secretary to bring us some coffee."

Scratching his head in bemusement, Quinn took the chair. "Little Kathleen Kerns with her own secretary," he said while his eyes lingered on her face. "I'll get used to it. Just give me a minute."

He was teasing her as he always had, and Kathleen's cheeks colored. She stabbed at a button on the phone. "Renee, we'd like coffee, please." While they waited, she leaned back in her chair and appraised him. "I was under the impression you kept your nose to the grindstone. How did you get so tan?"

"I was in Greece recently—I still do a lot of the buying for the stores. And I manage to play golf two or three times a week with business associates." He lit a cigarette and studied her through a curl of smoke. A touch of devilment kindled in his eyes. "It's a dirty job, but somebody has to do it."

"Right." She glanced toward the door as Renee entered, bearing a tray that held two mugs of coffee, sugar and cream. "Thanks, Renee."

The secretary set the tray on the desk, within reach of both Kathleen and Quinn, and left. Quinn took his coffee black, as did Kathleen.

He looked around for an ashtray, and she pushed one toward him. He tilted the cigarette in it and reached for his coffee. "You don't smoke?"

"I quit."

He gave her a wry smile. "Smart. I keep saying I'm going to. Maybe you can give me some pointers."

"Cold turkey. It's the only way."

He cradled the mug in his long, tanned fingers. Finding the stilted conversation unbearable, he blurted, "I'm sorry about your folks, Kathleen...and Patrick. I tried to write sympathy notes several times, but I never could make them sound right."

Kathleen's father had died of a second heart attack in the February of her senior year in high school, and they'd received word that Patrick had been killed in action in Vietnam eighteen months later. After that, Kathleen's mother had lost all desire to go on. Over the next few years, while Kathleen was in college, she became a vague, shadowy woman whom Kathleen couldn't reach. She had no appetite, no interest in anything, and the doctors were unable to help her. She finally died a few weeks before Kathleen received a master's degree in business administration. Because it had seemed to Kathleen that her mother had been dying for years, the funeral had been oddly anticlimactic.

"It all happened a long time ago," Kathleen said quietly. And much more happened than you know, Quinn, she reflected. "How is your mother?"

"She died in '83."

"I'm sorry."

He gazed into his coffee mug as he lifted it. "At least I was able to give her some of life's comforts during her last years." He took a swallow and set the mug down. His eyes returned to her face, and he said, "We're the only ones left, Kathleen."

She wondered what he was thinking as he uttered the words in that pensive tone.

"Maybe there's a meaning in that," he added, still with the same strange inflection.

Something in his manner disturbed her. The old feelings she'd had for him as a teenager stirred inside her and were instantly colored with bitterness. All these years she'd told herself that he'd been too drunk to remember what happened the night before he left for Vietnam. If he'd remembered, surely he would have contacted her at some point during the past fifteen years. Unless that night had meant nothing to him. It had to be one or the other. Either he didn't remember, or he remembered and it didn't matter. He'd been living in the same town with her for a year, and this was the first time he'd made any effort to see her. That could hurt her even now, if she let it. Amazing.

"I doubt it," she said flatly. "We're not that important in the scheme of things."

One sandy brow rose quizzically. "Importance is relative. You and your family were the most important people in my life once."

His words might have been an invitation for a stroll down memory lane, but she had no intention of taking it. She finished her coffee and set the mug back on the tray. The gesture was a clear communication that the chitchat was at an end. "As I said, it was a long time ago. What is it you want to see me about, Quinn?"

Illogically, the deliberate way she shifted the conversation was a sharp disappointment to him. He'd had a valid reason for making the appointment, but he wasn't kidding himself that he hadn't thought about renewing old acquaintanceships, too. After all, he could have contacted the congressman directly, or even Drewly, Smythe's man in Washington, but his business had provided an excuse to see *Kathleen*. After so much time he'd felt he needed an excuse. But he could see that she didn't want to reminisce.

He'd meant it when he said she'd changed. There was little of the happy, carefree Kathleen he remembered. She was thinner, but at the same time her body had acquired riper, more womanly curves. She was even more beautiful than she had been at seventeen, but along with the beauty there was an aura of untouchability. Hell, what had he expected? He knew she wasn't married, but she was probably involved in what the women's magazines called "a meaningful relationship." You couldn't ever go back. Whatever had made him think he could? He might as well state his business and leave.

He reached into his shirt pocket and pulled out a scrap of paper. "I know Congressman Smythe's been instrumental in bringing several Amerasian children from Vietnam to this country. There's somebody I want him to get out. An eleven-year-old boy. His name is Van Thieu." He placed the paper on her desk. The boy's name, along with several others, was printed on it. "He's living with his grandparents in the country, about thirty miles north of Saigon. Those are the grandparents' names below his, and the name of their village."

Kathleen stared at the foreign words in bewilderment. She had speculated on numerous reasons why Quinn might have contacted the congressman's office, but nothing remotely like this had entered her mind. It was true that Smythe had been successful in arranging for several Amerasian children to immigrate, but in those cases...

"Since the diplomatic channels broke down, it's not easy," she said, looking up at Quinn. "The other children were in orphanages. They had no family in Vietnam, and it was the father or other close relatives who wanted to bring them to the U.S. This boy is living with his grandparents. You're asking the Vietnamese authorities to take him away from them."

"That's right," he said, with a hard edge to the words.

"You'd better have an excellent reason or they won't even listen."

"I do," he said sharply, with conviction. "He's my son."

The words were like a blow to Kathleen's solar plexus. She sat stunned, unable to speak for a moment. The cruel irony of it created a knot of tears in her throat. If she opened her mouth, she would sob.

Fortunately it wasn't necessary for her to speak right away. Quinn went on talking. "I don't even know how much money I've spent over the past ten years, trying to find him and his mother. They were in Saigon when it fell in '75. After I gave up on government channels, I hired four different investigators, but nobody could find a trace of them until a few weeks ago."

Anger and determination underlined his words. As Kathleen listened, her bitterness grew. For ten years, against impossible odds, he'd kept on searching for a Vietnamese woman and the child they'd had together, while Kathleen had been struggling to put back together a life he'd destroyed. She would have given anything to have had a tiny fraction of his concern when *she*'d borne his baby. She'd *needed* him—needed *somebody*—when she'd become an unwed mother at seventeen and everyone close to her had been telling her that she had to give the baby away.

She closed her eyes briefly to shut out the sight of him and to compose herself. He doesn't know about Lauren, she told herself, but it didn't seem to help. At last she was composed enough to risk looking at him again.

She reached for a pen and notepad. Her hand shook, and she gripped the pen until her fingers ached. She called on every scrap of self-control she had. "I'll need as many details as you can give me. The mother's name, where she was living when you lost contact with her...."

The pain in her hand told her to loosen her grip on the pen. She concentrated on doing so while she went on talking, her voice emotionless and cold. A part of her mind noticed this with mild interest; it was as if a stranger were speaking and writing down the answers he gave to her questions. As quickly as she could, she brought the meeting to a close. "I'll relay this information to Congressman Smythe. I'll get back to you as soon as there's anything to report."

She had grown even more businesslike and distant as the meeting progressed, and Quinn was baffled by it. In spite of his decision not to be, he was disappointed by her attitude. Hurt, too—and yes, angry. What had happened to the Kathleen he'd known? She had to be in there somewhere, and he finally admitted to himself that he wanted to force her to reveal herself. He remained seated, watching her.

"My secretary always knows where to reach me," he said.

"Fine. You'll be hearing from us."

He continued to watch her, and she shifted uncomfortably in her chair. She looked at him.

"How late do you work?"

The unexpected question further unsettled her. "It—it depends."

"On what?"

She shrugged slightly. "How much work I have to do, and how pressing it is."

He received the sudden impression that her life was mostly work, that the social aspect of it was meager. The idea both saddened and encouraged him. "It's after five. Would you have dinner with me?"

She hesitated a beat before she replied, "I already have a dinner engagement. We have reservations at Giorgio's at seven." She knew, even as she said it, that she named the place and time to lend credence to her refusal. She wouldn't want him to think she'd fabricated plans on the spur of the moment simply because she didn't want to have dinner with him. He might want to know why, and she couldn't explain.

She was glad she had a valid excuse. If he assumed her date was with a man, so much the better.

You were wrong about her social life, Quinn told himself as he stifled his disappointment. "I'll expect to hear from you soon. Goodbye, Kathleen."

She wasn't aware how much tension she'd been under until he closed the door and she sagged in her chair. She felt limp and exhausted. Dear heaven, why did he have to come to her about his son? She wasn't sure she could deal with it. But she would have to find a way; it was her job. She reached for the phone, then realized that there probably wouldn't be anyone in the Washington office at this time of day. She would handle it tomorrow morning, after she'd had a night's sleep.

She dialed a local number. "Mary, it's Kathleen Kerns. I wanted to touch base with you. Is dinner still on for tonight?" Mary Denning was an interior decorator for one of the city's large furniture stores. They'd met when Mary helped Kathleen choose the furnishings for her duplex, and a casual friendship had developed between them. They talked on the telephone every month or so. During a conversation several weeks ago, they'd set a date for tonight's dinner.

There was a moment's silence on the other end of the line. Then Mary said, "Oh, Kathleen, I'm sorry...."

"You forgot."

"I didn't write it down, and last week, when my department manager invited me to a party he's giving . . . well, I'd hate to bow out on him this late, since he's my boss and all.''

"Of course you would. Don't worry about it. We'll do it another time."

Kathleen hung up just as Renee knocked and opened the door. "You need anything before I go home?"

Kathleen shook her head. "No, see you tomorrow."

Heavy silence fell over the office after Renee left. Kathleen considered going home, but it would be silent there, too. She decided to get some work done before leaving. It soon became obvious, however, that she couldn't concentrate on work. She kept thinking about Quinn and his Vietnamese lover. What had happened to her? Was Quinn still trying to find her? Since he hadn't volunteered the information, she hadn't wanted to ask. How long had they been together? she wondered. Had he known her before being captured by the Vietcong, or only after his escape? Foolishly, she found it more palatable to believe he hadn't met the woman before his capture, which had been only two months after his arrival in Vietnam. It hurt too much to imagine him with another woman so soon after the night of love that had become a watershed in her life. Before that night she had been naive and optimistic; afterward she'd had to face some of life's cruelest realities alone, and her silly belief that everything would eventually come right for her and

Quinn had died in the struggle merely to get through each day.

After seeing him again, she was more convinced than ever that he didn't remember that night. It had meant so little to him that his mind had thrown it away, and he'd taken a Vietnamese lover and had a son with her. Kathleen couldn't even tell herself that it had been a wartime fling, easily forgotten when he came home, as so many relationships between American soldiers and Vietnamese women had been. Quinn had spent ten years trying to find her; a man didn't go to that much trouble unless he cared deeply for a woman.

Still, she found it difficult to picture. Her image of Quinn had been formed fifteen years ago—a good-looking, fun-loving young man who excelled at sports. The combination had made him well liked by both sexes, and he'd enjoyed his popularity. An all-American boy. She recalled the Asian women she'd seen—fragile, retiring, cloaked in mystery. Not the sort of woman to attract Quinn, she would have thought. With a faintly sardonic smile, she emptied the ashtray he had used. Then she picked up his empty coffee mug and ran her finger along the rim his mouth had touched. She didn't even know the man Quinn Gresham had become.

No more than he knew the woman who was Kathleen Kerns. Kathleen's vision was misted with unwanted tears. She set the mug aside and brushed them away, despising herself for her weakness. It was over between you and Quinn fifteen years ago, she lectured herself. It never really began. Tears are wasted on what might have been.

Resolutely, she reached for the report she had been studying when Quinn arrived, and began to read. It was six-twenty by the time she had finished and dictated a memo to the congressman, outlining the relevant information.

She left the office and got into her car, mentally inventorying the contents of her refrigerator. Not much there that sounded appetizing. As she turned into the street, she remembered that she had failed to cancel the reservation at Giorgio's. She could go there alone and have a hot meal. By the time she got home, it would be too dark to see the flowers in the rock garden. That was fine, because she wasn't in the mood to appreciate them tonight, not without stirring up old memories again.

Giorgio's, then, she decided.

You can still forget this crazy idea and go home, Quinn told himself as he whipped the luxurious sedan into a parking spot at the curb. It was six-thirty—too early. He leaned back against the leather seat to wait and smoke a cigarette.

He still found it disconcerting when he tried to identify the cool, reserved businesswoman he'd met that afternoon with the sweet, lovable girl he remembered. Something about it didn't feel right. Perhaps that's why he'd followed his impulse to have dinner at Giorgio's tonight. Maybe if he saw her with someone else away from the office, he mused, she'd be more relaxed and he'd get a glimpse of the girl from his past. With a quiet chuckle Quinn took a drag on his cigarette. He was rationalizing. He was here because he'd left the evening free in case Kathleen agreed to dinner, and he was curious as hell to see the man she'd chosen over him.

While one part of him disliked being turned down, another part was glad she was seeing somebody. Obviously he hadn't spoiled something precious for her, as he once had feared. He'd tried several times to write to her after he got to Nam, to apologize for taking advantage of her schoolgirl crush and claiming her virginity on their last night together. But he never found the words that would let him say he was sorry without sounding as though she'd disappointed him, which couldn't have been further from the truth. At twenty-one he'd been more sheltered than he'd realized, but he'd been older and more experienced than she, and she'd trusted him. All the Kerns family had trusted him. He'd betrayed that trust, and he'd hated himself for it. Yet the memory of that night had made it just possible to get through two years of imprisonment by the Vietcong without losing his sanity. Whenever he'd thought he was going to crack, he'd retreated into his mind to be with Kathleen.

Now that he'd seen her again, he was glad he hadn't inflicted his guilty conscience on her. She had survived without apparent trauma. Finally he could stop castigating himself.

He waited until ten of seven before he left his car. The smell of honeysuckle wafted on the air as he reached for the door of the restaurant. A redhead dressed in filmy white and dripping with gold chains was exiting as he entered. She slowed her spike-heeled stride long enough to execute a lazy-eyed survey of Quinn's body and lean face, finally catching his glance with her green eyes. He returned her speculative look with an acknowledging smile and held the door open for her as she passed through. For reasons that were incomprehensible to him, women found him attractive. He was used to their subtle, or not so subtle, messages informing him of the fact. Come to think of it, it had been a good while since he'd accepted an implied invitation such as the redhead had just extended.

Must be getting old, he reflected, as he saw the hostess approaching.

Kathleen lingered over a glass of white wine before ordering dinner, drawing out the preliminaries as long as possible. The buzz of conversations all around her made her feel less alone. She perused the menu slowly as she sipped her wine. After she ordered, she settled back to people-watch with a second glass of wine. Playing the game of trying to guess the occupations of those at neighboring tables gave her something to do until her salad arrived.

The restaurant was full, and there was plenty of material for speculation. That red-faced man in the loud checked jacket was a traveling salesman, she decided. Probably sold oil field equipment. The suave, white-haired man to her right was a boardroom type. The voluptuous blonde with him was his mistress. Bold of the old dog to bring her to a popular restaurant. Maybe his wife was out of town, or maybe she just didn't care.

Kathleen's gaze wandered farther afield. Across the room, at a choice table next to a window, a man in a dark jacket sat alone, his face turned away from her. At the same instant that her mind realized that he looked familiar, he turned his head and gazed directly into her eyes.

Quinn!

She looked away quickly as heat flared in her face. It couldn't be a coincidence. She'd told him where she was having dinner, and he'd come to spy on her!

Chapter Three

Have you been stood up?''

She had been aware of Quinn's eyes on her for several minutes before he came over to her table. They were the longest minutes she had ever lived through. If she hadn't already ordered, she would have left. Instead, she'd had to sit there and burn with embarrassment and frustration.

He looked like one of those rugged male models in *Country Gentleman* in a navy blazer and white, open-collared shirt. He stood before her, at ease, his hands clasped on the back of a chair.

Kathleen's eyes were hot. "What are you doing here?" she countered. "And don't tell me you just happened to be in the neighborhood!"

He laughed, a low rumble. "No, I came because I knew you'd be here." The softening of his voice didn't calm her; it made her angrier. She wouldn't have him feeling sorry for her!

She narrowed her eyes. "To spy on me?"

"I wouldn't put it that way." Quinn's eyes beneath the lowered brows still held a hint of laughter.

She tossed an errant strand of hair back from her face. "How would you put it, then?"

He studied her in silence. Color stained her cheeks. Her eyes were like a dark, raging sea. He decided to ignore the challenge in her question. "I've already answered two questions. It's your turn."

The statement was like a gauntlet thrown at her feet. She could pick it up and try to keep her dignity intact, or ignore it and be thought a coward. Kathleen found it maddening. She stared at him stonily.

His left brow arched in what might have been derision or impatience. He shrugged and lifted both hands, palms up, in an exaggerated gesture. "Look, don't take it out on me because your date didn't show."

"I haven't been stood up," she said between her teeth. "Business forced us to change our plans. Not that it's any business of yours."

"My, aren't we snappy tonight?"

"I didn't ask you to come here."

"True." Her rudeness didn't ruffle him in the least. He swept an idle glance over the restaurant. "Looks like we're in the same boat. I could join you and let some of those hungry-looking people waiting in the vestibule have my table.'' His gaze returned to her stormy eyes, and he gave her a lopsided grin. "It's no fun, eating alone.''

"It will probably be even less fun for you eating at this table.''

Tucking his hands into the pockets of his gray trousers, he rocked gently on his heels, that easy, boyish grin still in place. Then he pulled out a chair. "I'll chance it.'' Without giving her an opportunity to refuse, he called the waiter over and announced that he was switching tables.

"No problem, Mr. Gresham,'' the waiter said. "You see how busy we are tonight. It's considerate of you to give up your table, sir. May I bring you a cocktail?''

"Scotch on the rocks.''

Kathleen sagged in defeat as she watched the waiter hurry away. "Considerate is hardly the word I'd use to describe your little maneuver, Quinn. Pushy, I'd call it.'' She glared at him, daring him to deny it.

The insult ran off Quinn like water off a steep roof. He preferred her anger to the indifference she'd exhibited at her office. "What's a little pushiness between old friends?'' he drawled. "I thought I was doing you a favor. You looked lonely over here.''

"I wasn't. And if you want to do me a favor, Quinn, don't do me any favors.''

She wasn't giving an inch, he thought, amused. Obviously she was embarrassed because he'd caught her having dinner alone. She was beautiful even when she was seething. He wondered if the guy she had planned to have dinner with appreciated her as he should. The waiter brought Quinn's drink, and Kathleen refused a third glass of wine.

"There's nothing to be embarrassed about, you know. If it was business, he probably had no choice but to break your date."

He meant it as consolation, but she didn't take it that way. "Who's embarrassed?" she sputtered. The nerve of the man!

He took a swallow of his drink and lit a cigarette. The smoke drifted across the table. "This is the non-smoking section," Kathleen informed him.

Slowly he considered her and took another drag on the cigarette before he crushed it out. "Does the smoke bother you?"

"Obviously. That's why I sit in the nonsmoking section. It's a dirty habit. I never realized that until I quit." God, she sounded like a self-righteous prig. She was, she admitted, trying to pick a fight.

The corners of his mouth twitched. "Why do all reformed smokers want to convert every smoker in sight? It's a real pain in the derriere."

"I thought you wanted to quit."

"When I decide to."

"If I make you uncomfortable, you can leave. You invited yourself to sit here," she reminded him sweetly. "I was looking forward to a nice, peaceful meal."

He refused to take the bait. Calmly he sipped his drink. By the time their salads arrived Kathleen was quite hungry. She ate and tried to ignore Quinn, who watched her as though he knew a secret about her. Finally he asked, "Who is he, Kathleen?"

She looked up startled. "Who?"

"The man you were supposed to have dinner with tonight."

She stiffened perceptibly. "That's still none of your business." For the first time she thought she detected a flicker of temper in his eyes. Her own indignation forced her to ignore it. "You always did have a colossal nerve, Quinn. I used to think it was cute. Now it's merely outrageous."

Enough is enough, Quinn thought. Exerting an effort of will, he controlled his temper. With a quiet, deliberate intensity, he stared at her. "I'm just curious to know who's warming your bed these days." He regretted the words the moment they were out. She'd been spoiling for a fight ever since he'd sat down, but that didn't excuse him.

The deliberate, brazen insult stunned her. It was unforgivable, even if she had asked for it. She hated him in that moment. "That's it!" Brown eyes blazing, she threw her napkin on the table and started to rise.

He half stood and caught her wrist. "Don't go, Kathleen. I apologize. That was a cheap shot."

"You're damned right it was!"

"Finish your dinner. Please."

Her eyes locked with his for long seconds, and then she lowered herself slowly into her chair. She felt a strong need to justify herself, and it infuriated her. She cleared her throat. "I'm only staying because it's silly to leave hungry." She felt better when she heard the cool, impersonal timbre of her voice. Beneath the table, her knees were trembling.

He watched her for a moment before finishing his salad. When the waiter brought their entrées, Kathleen wondered if she'd made a mistake in staying. She was hungry, but she would have to swallow past the humiliating lump in her throat.

Quinn made an effort to defuse the tension that hung over the table like a heavy, black cloud. "I know it's no excuse, but for a while tonight I sort of fell through a time warp. That's why I asked about your date. I felt an overpowering urge to check him out, to see if he passed muster—like when we were kids."

Kathleen let her eyes meet his. She made a humorless sound. "My goodness, I wonder how I've survived all these years without your protection."

His eyes were suddenly narrow and probing. "I don't know," he responded gravely. "How have you?"

"Very well, actually. There was nobody left to lean on, so I learned to make it on my own." Her voice was even, assured. It made the lie sound so much like the truth that she almost believed it herself.

"A loner, Kathleen?" he asked quizzically. "That doesn't sound like you."

"You don't really know me anymore, Quinn. Haven't you realized that yet?"

Maybe she was right. Fifteen years ago he couldn't have envisoned her as the competent, independent career woman she was today. But he didn't like hearing her say it. For one thing, he had caught a glimpse of vulnerability in her tonight, when she let that tough-lady mask slip a little. For another, he wanted—perhaps needed—to peel away the protective layers she had wound around herself and find the old Kathleen still intact. But he thought he'd better let up on her for now. She wasn't in a soul-baring mood. A new topic of conversation was called for.

"What's the procedure for bringing Van here to live?"

It was a moment before she realized that he wasn't going to answer her question. Instead he wanted to talk about his son. She had forgotten how his mind could leap from one topic to another without any transitions. She used to find it stimulating. Hurriedly she shifted mental gears to keep up with him. "These situations can be pretty touchy. I'm not sure how the congressman will handle it. My guess is that he'll ask somebody at the Australian embassy in Vietnam to talk to the grandparents unofficially. The Australians have been helpful in the past. Before Congressman Smythe gets officially involved, he'll want to know how the grandparents feel about letting the child go."

"I don't give a damn how they feel," he said grimly. "I want Van out of there."

It was the second time he had reacted with resentment when the grandparents were mentioned. Kathleen wondered if there were hard feelings between Quinn and his lover's parents. If so, they might well refuse to cooperate.

"Have you thought this through carefully, Quinn?"

"I've had ten years to think about it." He watched her cut into her halibut steak. "I'm sensing a distinct air of disapproval here. You've got a burr under your saddle. What is it?"

She put down her silverware and looked at him levelly. "Since you ask, you're not thinking of anybody but yourself. What you're proposing is selfish."

Her accusation engendered more surprise in him than anger. "How do you figure that?"

"Try to put yourself in Van's place. He's an eleven-year-old child, living with his grandparents. Suddenly his father, whom he doesn't know from Adam, enters the picture and wants to uproot him and take him to a foreign country to live. How would that make you feel?"

His jaw hardened. "It isn't my fault that he doesn't know me."

Kathleen sighed. "That's beside the point. The fact remains that he doesn't. Do you really believe he'll want to come and live with you? He'll be terrified. He'll probably end up hating you." She frowned as she searched for the right words. Suddenly it seemed vital to convince him. "Sometimes the best thing you can do for a child is give him up."

Somehow the past and the present were getting mixed up in Kathleen's mind. In a flash of memory, she heard her mother's angry voice: Pure selfishness, Kathleen, that's what it is! How are you going to raise a baby by yourself? Don't count on us to help you, because we can't.

Kathleen had wanted to hurt her mother in return. I've learned not to count on you for much of anything, Mother, she'd flung back.

Quinn had been ready to tell her curtly to mind her own business, but then he saw the stricken look on her face. He didn't understand why she was so worked up over a child she'd never even seen. "You don't understand," he said, striving for patience. "Van's grandparents care nothing for him. They've taken him out of school, and they send him to work in the rice paddies every day. In return for the food he eats, they've got a full-time laborer. That's the only reason they let him stay around."

Kathleen was staring in disbelief. She had paled as he spoke, and now she asked faintly. "How do you know this?"

"It's in the report the investigator sent me, and a lot more, too."

"But he's only eleven!"

"And there's a good possibility he won't live to be much more than that if I don't get him out of there."

There must be some mistake, Kathleen thought. "I find it hard to believe they'd treat their own grandchild worse than a—a slave."

"I know you do. You haven't seen what it's like over there. Nobody can understand who hasn't been there. They probably don't even claim him as a grandchild. They disowned his mother before he was born. Van is a shame and an embarrassment to them. If they didn't need him to work in the fields, they wouldn't allow him in their sight."

"Oh." It was beginning to make sense to her. She'd been so eager to discredit Quinn's motives that she hadn't given him a chance to explain. She realized now what he was driving at. "I suppose illegitimacy is a much worse stigma over there than here."

He was studying Kathleen's face as if to see into her mind. "Van isn't illegitimate. I was married to his mother." He spoke quietly, yet with a reluctance that confused Kathleen. "The stigma is his mixed blood."

Kathleen gaped at him, wondering how many more surprises he had in store for her. It was stupid to be hurt by the fact that Quinn had married somebody else, but she was. It was worse than knowing he had taken a lover. In time she might have been able to convince herself that a love affair could only have happened in the hell of war, that he'd needed the softness and comfort of a woman to get through it. But he had married the woman, and Quinn would never have married somebody he didn't love.

She managed to find her voice. "I'm sorry. I assumed..." She broke off, not knowing how to finish without making things worse. Flustered, she looked down at her hand, which rested beside her plate.

"Kathleen?"

She forced herself to meet his eyes. He smiled and before she was aware of his intention he reached across the table and took her hand in both of his. There was an odd gentleness in his manner, as if he knew he'd hurt her.

Ignoring her sharp jerk of surprise, he let his eyes roam over her shining hair and pause to comtemplate her soft mouth. There was a deeply buried core of sensuality in her, he thought suddenly. She tried to hide it, but her mouth gave her away. He had to fight back an urge to lean across the table and kiss her. "Will you do something for me?" he asked softly.

Tremors skipped over her skin, as if a cool breeze had caressed it. The sensation was emanating from the hand that was still trapped in both of Quinn's. "What?"

"Don't make any more assumptions about me. Things aren't always what they seem."

The words made no sense to her. Was he trying to tell her something without really telling her? That made no sense, either. She looked down, strangely moved by the warmth being created within the co-coon of his hands. She twirled the stem of her wine-glass with her free hand and watched the light from the chandelier play on the elegant crystal bowl. She had to know about his wife, she realized, no matter what the truth was. Without looking up, she said, "Are you still searching for Van's mother?"

"No."

She looked up then into eyes that were blurred with sadness. He released her hand to down the last of his whiskey. They had both abandoned their meals half-eaten, and Quinn pushed his plate back in order to rest his forearms on the table, as if he needed the support of something solid before he went on. He kept his eyes steady on hers.

"Mai was killed when Saigon fell. After so long, when I could find no trace of her, I suspected that was what happened. But my suspicions weren't confirmed until three weeks ago, when I received the last investigator's report." He paused to catch the waiter's eye and order another drink. It was obvious that he found it difficult to talk about his wife.

When he'd swallowed some of the fresh drink, he continued. "I'd left the country with my division weeks earlier, and I was trying to work through the red tape to bring her and Van to the States before South Vietnam was overrun. Most of the Vietnamese seemed to think Saigon could hold out indefinitely. They'd lived with that war so long, I guess they couldn't envision anything changing. I wanted Mai to take the baby and go to the American embassy when I left, but she refused."

He looked away for a moment, as though to gather his strength. When his eyes returned to hers, they held a resolve to say what had to be said. "She probably tried to get out during the final evacuation. I'll never know for sure. At any rate, she got separated from Van. That was easy to do in the chaos. I talked to a pilot who flew a cargo plane in the airlift during the final days before Saigon's surrender. He said it was a madhouse. Many families were separated. From what the investigator could piece together, she was knocked down and trampled by a mob of hysterical refugees. Van ended up in an orphanage. There was no way to identify him, so they called him Van Thieu. His grandparents finally decided to look for him when he was old enough to work in the fields. Van lived in the orphanage until they took him out a few months ago. They probably identified him by the odd-shaped birthmark he had on his right thigh.''

The human tragedy behind his brief account made Kathleen feel like weeping. She slid her hand across the table and curled her fingers over the back of his hand. ''Quinn, I'm so sorry.''

His face was set and still, but there was torment in the convulsive strength with which his fingers gripped hers. ''Sometimes I think the horror of that war will never end,'' he muttered.

''I know,'' she said softly.

''I went over there with a head full of childish idealism. I was captured by the Vietcong.... It didn't take them long to knock the idealism out of me.''

''We heard only that you were missing in action. It must have been—''

''It's ancient history.'' His words sliced off her attempt at sympathy. ''What I'm saying is that the Vietnam war was evil. It took Patrick and Mai ... and it scares hell out of me to think about what it's done to Van.'' Something flickered over his face, and she thought he was starting to say something more, then changed his mind. He released her fingers and raked a hand through his hair. "I'm ready to get out of here. What about you?"

"Yes."

When he called the waiter over, she insisted on paying half the check. "I came here on my own," she told him. "There's no reason why you should pay for my dinner."

He didn't agree with her, she could tell, but he gave in. Talking about Mai and his imprisonment had drained him, she thought; he didn't have the energy to insist on his own way.

As they left the restaurant, he took her arm. "I may have let you pay for your own dinner, and I know you're a liberated woman and all that…but I'm going to see you to your car. Where is it?"

"On the south side of the restaurant," she told him as they reached the shadowy sidewalk. Her high heels clicked on the pavement as he slipped his arm around her shoulders. The thought of pulling away from him flitted through her mind and drifted away.

He flicked a sidelong glance at her. "What, no feminist harangue?"

"No," she said, smiling. "I'm grateful for your company, actually. It's pretty dark in this parking lot." His arm over her shoulders felt friendly.

"Well, well, well." There was amusement in his voice.

"That's my car, over there." She tilted her head and tossed back her hair, unaware that she had moved closer to him.

The space between her car and the one next to it was so narrow that Quinn had to drop back and walk behind her. She turned around to thank him for escorting her and discovered that he was closer than she'd thought. With a quick intake of breath, Kathleen tried to step back, but the car stopped her. His dark jacket and tanned face blended with the night, but his eyes caught the faint, filtered light from the restaurant. They seemed to glow from within, like bright embers. For an instant Kathleen felt an eerie displacement, as though they had been whisked away to some uninhabited spot. The restaurant and the busy street receded. His burning eyes, the shadowed planes and angles of his face, the scar faintly seen on his right cheek, all made him seem hard and relentless, a more primitive being than the man who had shared her dinner.

"What are you thinking?" Even his voice sounded different, more demanding, more compelling.

All at once Kathleen realized that she was holding her breath. She released it slowly. It was the darkness that was playing tricks on her, she told herself, the darkness that gave her this sense of danger that made her tremble. "Nothing very profound," she said lightly. "Just that I should have been in my office, catching up with work, instead of wasting an hour in a restaurant."

"It wasn't wasted—not for me," he said as he stood gazing down at her. "I'm glad your date couldn't make it."

The undercurrents she sensed in his admission made her pulse speed up. She should tell him that her "date" had been a woman and not even a close friend, but she'd left him with his false assumption too long for it to have been anything but intentional. It wasn't important for him to know, she told herself. She probably wouldn't see him again, anyway. "Are you?" Worried that he could see the effect his nearness was having on her, she closed her eyes and leaned back against the car.

"Kathleen..."

She opened her eyes and met his. Slowly, deliberately, he lifted his arms and placed his hands on the top of her car, leaning down and bringing his face close to hers. She tried to laugh, so he would know she wasn't so easily unsettled. After all, she was an adult now and could meet him on his own terms. But the laugh came out sounding more like a croak. "I have to go."

He didn't move. She could feel his warm breath on her cheek. "Not until you admit you're glad I showed up tonight."

She did laugh then, nervously. "I'll do no such thing!"

He shifted and she thought, Thank heaven, he's going to let me go. But instead of leaving her, he cupped his hand around the back of her neck. "You don't have to say it with words."

She managed a startled "What?" before he dipped his head and brought his mouth down to hers.

The kiss was light at first, not really serious, a mere brushing of lips. In fact, she thought the deep, throaty sound Quinn made was a chuckle; he was teasing her. She was still in control, and she thought she could have held on until he lifted his head, could have passed it off with a joke and a laugh—if he hadn't taken the opportunity to slide the moist tip of his tongue between her lips.

Kathleen stiffened with shock. She could neither breathe nor think, and for one roaring instant her heart stopped. When it resumed beating her pulse hammered and her blood heated and her limbs gave up their rigidity. The roaring in her ears became a wild cadence that shut out everything but Quinn.

In one exploding instant she lost control, and Quinn was no longer teasing. Suddenly their mouths were hot and hungry and demanding. Kathleen's arms found their way around his neck, while Quinn's arms crushed her slender body in a passionate embrace. The kiss deepened as their mutual need refused to be denied, then deepened again. It went on endlessly as their bodies pressed together in a blind instinctive seeking. The only sounds in the soft April night were of labored breathing and moans muffled by mouths that could not get enough of each other.

Kathleen's senses were reeling with the taste and smell and feel of him, and still she could not get enough. She plunged her fingers into the curling hair at the nape of his neck and tilted her head back to deepen the kiss. His tongue plundered the intimacy of her mouth, and his hands slid down to cup her hips and pull her lower body against his. The straining, masculine hardness of him set her blood on fire. Desperately she took his bottom lip between her teeth. Uttering a groan of mingled pain and pleasure, Quinn crushed her to him in a convulsion of fierce need. She could feel him struggling to regain control, and finally his bruising grip on her body loosened, and his kiss became gentle and clinging. When at last he lifted his head, Kathleen's breath escaped in a soft sound of pleasure.

She tilted her head back and gazed up at him in silence, her fingers toying with the hair that curled down over his collar. His eyes were deep and dark with mystery. He drew in a ragged breath and splayed his fingers on her shirt beneath the back of her jacket. They might have been the only two people within a hundred miles. For Kathleen, nothing existed in that moment but Quinn and the uncontrollable emotions his kiss had unleashed in her.

With an odd little smile he slid one hand from beneath her jacket and brushed his knuckles along the line of her jaw. Sighing, she turned her head so that her cheek rested against his hand. His knuckles were hard and hair-roughened, and the contact sent a comforting warmth trickling through her.

She might have stood there all night in a dreamy haze if a driver, pulling out of the parking lot, hadn't sounded his horn and shattered the gossamer night. She started at the sound, and shuddered as she let her arms fall to her side.

"What are we doing?" she asked in a small voice, sounding frightened and disoriented, like somebody waking up in an unfamiliar place. She couldn't meet his eyes.

"Making out is, I think, the current vernacular," he said dryly. He brushed his knuckles beneath her chin, lifting it and forcing her to look at him. "Nice, huh?"

"I'm not sure," she said vaguely.

"You thought it was nice a few minutes ago, don't deny it."

She sighed. "I'm not denying it. That's not what I meant."

"What then?"

She shook her head. "I don't like not being in control. It scares me."

He rubbed his thumb across the fullness of her bottom lip and laughed. "You're still the same funny Kathleen. I'm relieved. I was beginning to think she'd gone away somewhere and left a total stranger in her body."

She couldn't see the humor in it. He trailed his fingers lightly down her throat. It made her skin quiver. She thought she might cry if she didn't get away from him. She had felt like crying, in fact, a great deal of the time since Quinn's name had turned up on her desk yesterday. It made her angry. Quinn could still get to her emotions as no other man had ever done. After fifteen years, he could drop back into her life, kiss her once and immediately destroy what little sense she had where he was concerned. She took a deep, bracing breath.

"Quinn?"

"Hmm?"

"Was Mai very beautiful?"

His smile faded, and his fingers on her throat stilled. He looked down at her with an irritated expression. "I don't remember anymore," he said finally. He reached behind her and opened her car door.

Glad to put more space between them, she slid into the driver's seat. Quinn bent down and kissed her lightly on the forehead. "Good night, Kathleen."

He slammed the door and watched her drive away.

Chapter Four

The lights were on in the other half of the duplex when Kathleen got home. Without unlocking her door first, she ran up Maggie's steps and rang the bell. The woman who opened the door was short and pleasantly plump. Her blond hair was generously streaked with silver.

"Welcome back, gadabout," Kathleen said.

Maggie grinned. "Hi. I've been watching for you. Come on in. I have something to show you."

"Let me guess. New pictures of Sara."

Maggie looked mischievously over her shoulder. "How'd you know?"

Kathleen said innocently, "Wild stab in the dark," and both women laughed.

Kathleen entered a living area similar to her own, except that Maggie's was furnished with dark, heavy antique pieces, brought back from foreign places where she had lived with her late husband. Dink Owens, dead now for more than four years, had been a pipeline construction foreman.

"Let me get the pictures," Maggie said, disappearing into the kitchen.

Kathleen sat down on the sofa and kicked off her shoes. Maggie returned with several photographs of a blond, blue-eyed toddler. Sara was Maggie's only grandchild, and Kathleen had been kept thoroughly informed of each tiny milestone in the little girl's life.

"Is she precious or what?" Maggie asked.

Kathleen spread the photographs on the coffee table. "How cute. Her hair has finally decided to grow!"

"She's talking a blue streak. Complete sentences, too. You should hear her."

"But she isn't even two yet. Isn't that a bit early for complete sentences?" Kathleen was sure Sara's sentences were of the "Dada hold" variety.

"What can I say?" Maggie's pride was unabashed. "The child is a genius."

Kathleen smiled. "That's my cue to say she takes after her grandmother."

Maggie gave her a deep laugh. "I've got you trained, haven't I? But it happens to be true that Sara takes after me. I keep telling my son-in-law that. Jeff claims she's like his side of the family."

Kathleen studied the photographs for another moment. As far as she could tell, Sara just looked like Sara. Occasionally Maggie's doting on Sara got to be a little much, but Kathleen would never let Maggie know she thought so. Sometimes, listening to Maggie go on about her daughter's family, Kathleen felt an unreasonable resentment of Ellen, who seemed to lead a charmed life. Ellen, who was Kathleen's age, had a challenging career as an officer in a Topeka bank, a bright, beautiful daughter and a loving husband. As far as Kathleen could tell, the only sorrow that had ever touched Ellen's life was the death of her father, and she'd had Jeff to comfort her in her loss. When such thoughts entered Kathleen's mind she pushed them away quickly, because she knew they were petty. Ellen, Jeff and Sara were the only family Maggie had left. Why wouldn't she be absorbed in their lives? Furthermore, Maggie had no way of knowing that whenever she talked about her granddaughter, Kathleen's heart twisted a little. How could she, when she knew nothing about the tragedy in Kathleen's past?

"Oh, well, Jeff is only Sara's father," Kathleen teased. "What does he know?"

"Yeah," Maggie agreed with seeming seriousness. "He's hardly an unbiased observer."

Kathleen tried to keep a straight face and couldn't. "As you are, of course."

Maggie chuckled. "Listen to me, will you? I used to swear I'd never be a bragging grandma, and I'm the worst of the lot. How do you stand me?"

"It's not a major fault," Kathleen told her. "Indifferent grandparents are worse." For an instant she saw her mother leaning over Lauren's crib for the first time, then walking away. She shook off the memory. "Didn't you stay in Topeka longer than you'd planned?"

"A couple of days. I was having so much fun babysitting Sara that I couldn't pull myself away. But when Jeff started fixing me up with men to get me out of the house evenings, I knew it was time to come home."

Kathleen folded her legs and rested her stockinged feet on the cushion beneath her. She propped one elbow on the sofa's wide, overstuffed arm and rested her cheek against her hand. "Jeff got you a date? How sweet." Her tone was mildly amused. "Tell me all about it."

An uncharacteristic red stained Maggie's face. "It wasn't exactly a date. The man was Jeff's father. He's divorced and semiretired. Jeff made it sound like I'd be doing him a favor, said his father was lonely." She grunted and made a sweeping gesture. "You know what a sucker I am for a sob story. Besides," she added defensively, "I was . . ."

"Interested," Kathleen supplied. "You're a healthy, vital woman, even if you are a grandma. And you should be flattered. Jeff paid you a compliment, asking you to go out with his father. What's his name?"

"Bert. Short for Robert. He owns two restaurants in Topeka, but he recently hired a manager to see to the day-to-day operations, and he has time on his hands."

"So, did you have a good time?"

"I didn't go out with Bert to have a good time," Maggie said too quickly. "I only went because Jeff asked me to."

Maggie had circumvented her question, Kathleen noted. "I'm sure Jeff appreciated that."

Maggie shrugged. "Well, I felt sorry for Bert, too. Jeff's mother is one of those bored, restless women who complain about everything. You know what I mean. If it rains when she's planned a picnic, it's a personal insult. Jeff works at having a relationship with both his parents, but his clearest memories of growing up are of his mother nagging his father and threatening about once a month to leave him. Finally she said it once too often, and Bert told her never mind, he'd find a place of his own and he'd expect to hear from her lawyer."

"Did Bert tell you that?"

"Oh, no, he's too much of a gentleman to criticize his ex-wife. Ellen told me."

Too much of a gentleman, eh? Kathleen thought. Maggie was more impressed with Bert than she was willing to admit. "Did Bert take you to one of his restaurants?"

"No." Maggie squirmed into a more comfortable position in her corner of the sofa. "He said he'd rather go someplace where he wasn't known, so we wouldn't be interrupted. To tell you the truth, I guess he felt as strange about the evening as I did. Two old codgers, dating..." Maggie shook her head.

"You stop that, Maggie Owens. You're not an old codger, and I'll bet Bert isn't either."

"He's sixty," Maggie said, "but he doesn't look it. He took me to a place with a dance floor. He's really an excellent ballroom dancer. So good that he made me seem light on my feet, and that's an accomplishment. Dink hated to dance, so I never got any practice." She frowned and then looked wistful over what must have been a memory of her husband. "Bert's not at all like Dink, that's for sure."

"That doesn't mean you can't enjoy his company, does it?"

Maggie bent over to place the photographs of Sara in a neat stack, as though her hands needed something to do. "We did have our children and Sara in common, so talking was easy." She laid down the stack of photographs and looked at Kathleen with a faintly puzzled expression. "But it seemed odd, Kathleen. I felt as though I shouldn't be having a good time with Bert, as though I were being disloyal to Dink's memory."

"You know that's nonsense." Kathleen tucked the hem of her skirt over her feet.

Maggie sighed. "My head knows it, but my heart..." Shaking off a quick moodiness, she cocked her head and smiled. "Anyway, Bert and I got to know each other a little better, and that's the end of it.

What about you? What have you been up to while I was gone, except working?"

"Dealing with a ghost from my past." Kathleen blurted out the words before she had time to weigh what she was saying.

Maggie's interest was engaged instantly. "Really? Male or female?"

"Male, but that's not important."

Maggie's expression was wide-eyed. "It's not?" She was having fun, now that the tables were turned.

"No, I was only uncomfortable because I hadn't seen him for fifteen years, and never expected to see him again. Then, all of a sudden, there he was in my office... and tonight he came to the restaurant where I was eating and asked to join me. It was weird."

"I see," Maggie commented. "Fifteen years ago you were a mere child. He must have made a terrific impression on you for you to remember him, much less be disturbed by his sudden appearance."

"I didn't say I was disturbed."

Maggie threw up her hands. "I stand corrected."

"He was older than I was," Kathleen went on. "And he was my brother's best friend." She was aware that she was attempting to defend herself as earnestly as Maggie had moments earlier. "I had an adolescent crush on him." She slid her feet off the sofa and put her shoes on. "Somehow the boys you were madly in love with in your teens usually turn out, when you see them later, to be fat and bald."

"But this one isn't?"

Kathleen's bemused smile gave away more than she realized. "No, Quinn is certainly not fat or bald. He's quite good-looking, in fact. And he's become very successful in business." She rose to her feet. "As I said, the whole thing was weird."

"Are you seeing him again?"

"Oh, no." Kathleen retrieved her purse. "I have no plans to see him again. I'll probably talk to him on the phone about something he wants the congressman to do for him, but that's it."

"Just a thought," Maggie said mildly. "I was hoping maybe you'd found the perfect man at last."

"The perfect man does not exist."

Maggie followed Kathleen to the door. "Come to think of it, a perfect man would probably bore the stuffing out of you. What you need, Kathleen, is a challenge."

Kathleen opened the door, then turned around to say, "A challenge, maybe, but I'm afraid Quinn would be a lot more than that." She stepped on the porch. "I'm glad you had fun at Ellen's, but it's nice to have you back. Why don't we have dinner soon?"

"Whenever you say."

"One day next week. I'll let you know." Kathleen shut Maggie's door, walked across the yard and unlocked her own. After being shut up all day, the place was stuffy. She turned on a light and opened some windows to let in the cool evening air. She slipped out of her shoes and jacket, then carried them to her bedroom, where she opened another window. With only moonlight for illumination, she undressed down to her panties and bra and stretched out on the bed.

Lying on her back, she put her hands behind her head and let the gentle night breeze flow over her. Her visit with Maggie had helped to put some distance between herself and what had happened with Quinn tonight, but not enough to prevent her from thinking about Quinn's kiss. Kathleen still wasn't sure how it had happened. One second she had been standing there in a crowded restaurant parking lot about to say a friendly good-night, the next, Quinn's lips touched hers and the whole world went crazy.

A momentary aberration. Except that the kiss had lasted much longer than a moment. Fool that she was, she had loved it, too. But her emotions had had nothing to do with the Quinn Gresham who had kissed her tonight; somehow Quinn and her feelings had become confused with a man and feelings that were fifteen years in the past. She would have to make sure it didn't happen again in the future.

If only there were somebody else she could pass Quinn along to, somebody else who could contact the congressman and handle the arrangements for bringing Quinn's son to America. Then she wouldn't have to see or talk to him: she wouldn't be so afraid that she might forget herself again....

Coward, she scolded herself. Following up on Quinn's request was her responsibility, and besides, there was no one else to do it. It would be good for her, she thought stoutly. Once she'd gotten used to talking to Quinn again, she'd realize that she'd been cured of her love for him long ago. Actually, she should be grateful for the chance to get rid of that old emotional garbage once and for all. It was long past time.

The first thing she did on reaching her office the next morning was phone Congressman Smythe's Washington office. She explained Quinn's request to Jeb Drewly, who seemed eager to be of help. "I'll talk to the congressman the minute he comes in," Jeb said. "Gresham is pretty important in Oklahoma."

"I suppose," Kathleen murmured.

"His company injects a good chunk of money into the state economy. Congressman Smythe will be happy for the opportunity to help."

Quinn would get a subtly worded request for a sizable contribution to Smythe's next campaign, Kathleen thought. The "You scratch my back, and I'll scratch yours" philosophy was what kept the political wheels greased; it was one of the things she liked least about the world of politics, even though she considered Jefferson Smythe a good and competent representative for his district.

"I'll start the ball rolling," Jeb was saying, "and get back to you."

Kathleen hung up and attacked the work on her desk. There was more than enough to keep her mind occupied all day. She didn't even take time out for lunch. Work was a wonderful defense against remembering.

What was that noise? Kathleen opened her eyes and they were immediately flooded by bright sunlight from her open bedroom window. Groaning, she pulled a pillow over her head and tried to ignore the insistent hammering on her front door. Whoever it was must have decided the bell wasn't loud enough. Maggie? No, Maggie would have called. But maybe her telephone was out of order.

The hammering continued. Obviously she wasn't going to get back to sleep. She threw the pillow at the wall. She had planned to sleep until noon, at least, to rest up from a work week of ten- and twelve-hour days. As her sleep-fogged mind cleared, she could see that plan going down the tube.

Mumbling furiously under her breath, she threw back the sheet and fumbled for her robe on the back of a chair. After an instant's pause, the knocking resumed. "I hope your knuckles are bleeding," Kathleen muttered as she tied the belt of her robe and staggered into the bathroom to splash cold water on her face. Straightening, she glanced at her sleepy-eyed reflection in the bathroom mirror. Her hair looked as if birds had made a nest in it during the night. She shrugged and turned away. "What you see is what you get," she said. Anybody who appeared at her door uninvited on Saturday morning deserved whatever he found.

"Hold your horses," she shouted as she headed for the door. "I'm coming!" She looked through the peephole in the front door. Quinn was staring impatiently back at her. She pulled open the door.

Quinn grinned. "It's about time. I thought you'd died in there."

Kathleen glared, thought about slamming the door in his face, reconsidered and said, "I was asleep. What do you want?"

"Good morning to you, too." Without waiting for an invitation, Quinn opened the storm door and stepped inside. Perfectly at ease, he gazed about her living room.

Fuming, Kathleen shut the door with more force than necessary and planted her hands on her hips. "It's Saturday, in case you hadn't noticed. I was planning to sleep in."

"You did." He walked over to a native American print on the wall for a closer look. Then he ran an approving glance over an Italian candy dish on a walnut table. "It's after nine." The place was spit-and-polish clean, the decor of no particular style but attractive, even elegant. Like Kathleen, he thought.

He looked rested and fit in khaki trousers and a blue knit shirt. She hadn't seen him for ten days, and it was hard to stifle the feeling of gladness that was pushing aside her irritability. Hands in his pockets, he wandered over to the atrium doors, where the view was a riot of daffodils and early-blooming irises. "Mmm, this is nice. Do you rent?"

Kathleen tugged the belt of her robe tighter. "The mortgage company and I own it."

"Good investment," he approved, turning to appraise her. He wondered if she had any idea how desirable she looked with her hair mussed and her lovely eyes still slightly glazed from sleep. He fought an urge to go to her, haul her against him and kiss her senseless. He wasn't sure why he had decided to barge in on her like this, but now that he was here, he was more sure than ever that the best way to handle Kathleen was with a careful, by-degrees approach. She was like a wary bird who would fly away at the first movement. He kept his hands in his pockets and his feet planted on the thick carpet.

"I'm thrilled you approve," she said, covering a yawn. "I don't know how I would have made it through the day if you hadn't come over to tell me that." She headed for the kitchen. "Now that you've splashed a little sunshine into my life, perhaps you should go out and look for little old ladies to help across the street."

"I can't leave," he replied mildly, following her and sliding onto a bar stool while she started coffee brewing. "My car died a couple of houses down the block. I need a new battery."

"Well, incredible as it seems, I don't happen to have one on hand." She flipped the switch on the automatic drip coffee maker. "Careless of me, I know. You can use my phone to call a garage."

"No hurry." He propped his elbows on the bar and gave her an amiable grin. "I need to talk to you. Any progress in Van's case?"

Frustrated, she ran a hand through her sleep-tousled hair. "I keep regular business hours at the office," she said curtly. "You could have phoned me any day this week." After the words were said, she realized they sounded as though she was disappointed that he hadn't called. Confused, she wondered if that were true.

"I was out of town."

"You've heard of long distance, I presume." Damn, she couldn't seem to shut up about the telephone.

"I never had the time until after ten at night. I was afraid I'd disturb you."

"But you don't mind disturbing me on Saturday morning?"

He shrugged. "I assumed you'd be up long before now. You used to be an early riser, as I recall."

"I told you—" She broke off. There was no point in pointing out again that she'd changed. It seemed to be wasted breath. She got two mugs from the cabinet. "The congressman is working on Van's case. When there's anything to report, you'll be the first to know." After a pause, she added grudgingly, "Would you like a cup of coffee before you leave?"

"Thanks." He watched her pour the coffee, thinking how soft and delectable her mouth was. It would be so easy to lean across and kiss her. He gripped his knees with his hands beneath the bar. "Do you have any cold cereal?"

She shook her head helplessly. "I don't believe this," she muttered. "Are you sure you wouldn't prefer eggs and bacon? A waffle perhaps?"

He wanted to touch her so badly that he forgot for the moment about caution. He reached over and cupped his hand around the side of her neck as she frowned and glared at him. "Cereal will do." His thumb rubbed lightly against the underside of her jaw. When she was in her robe and without makeup, it was easier for him to detect the sweet vulnerability he'd caught a fleeting glimpse of at Giorgio's. "You're lovely in the morning," he mused.

"If you think flattery will influence me to drive you somewhere for a battery," she managed as his thumb pressed lightly on her earlobe, "don't hold your breath." She stepped back out of his reach, opened a cabinet door and slapped a bowl and cereal boxes on the bar. "Cornflakes or raisin bran, that's all I have. I'm not running a short-order café here."

He picked up his coffee and appraised her over the rim of the mug. "I thought we could go out to the club and play a round of golf, then have lunch somewhere and pick up the battery on the way back."

"I hate golf," she stated rudely.

Smiling at her, he announced, "That's probably because you're no good at it. I'll give you a lesson."

She got the milk from the refrigerator and slammed it down in front of him. "I don't want a lesson!"

Pouring raisin bran into the bowl, he countered, "No problem. You can just walk the course with me. The exercise will be good for you."

Evidently she couldn't insult him. Sighing, she sat down across from him and reached for her coffee. She might as well drink it; she wasn't going to get any more sleep this morning, anyway. "I'd forgotten how persistent you can be." The coffee was just right. She took a second swallow.

"When I want something."

"I'd think you'd rather have another golfer along, or at least somebody who enjoys walking. I'm no good at sports. I go to a health spa and walk on a treadmill for half an hour three times a week. It's like taking medicine."

He chuckled and reached for the sugar bowl. "I don't care if you can't walk and chew gum at the same time, Kathleen. I just want to be with you. Besides, you'll like the golf course better than a treadmill. Take my word for it."

His unabashed insistence was breaking down her resistance, just as it had done at the restaurant last week. She gazed into her coffee. In truth, a walk around a manicured golf course on a nice April morning didn't sound half bad. And she had nothing planned all day except for dinner with Maggie at seven. She gave him a thoughtful look. "I don't get it, Quinn. Why me?"

He raised an eyebrow as he poured milk on his cereal. "That's easy. You're a beautiful, intelligent woman." He paused, watching a frown furrow her brow. "And we go back a long way. We used to have a very special relationship; at least, I thought we did."

She didn't know what he meant by "a very special relationship," and she was afraid to ask. She rose quickly. "I'm not sure people should ever try to resurrect the past. They're almost certain to be disillusioned."

He watched her move restlessly to the cabinet, forget why she'd opened the door and shut it again. "Okay, I'll buy that." He sipped his coffee calmly. "How about if we pretend we just met and go from here?"

With a quick flash of brown eyes, she whirled on him. "It isn't that simple."

Baffled by her sudden burst of temper, he eyed her meditatively and took another swallow of coffee. "How do you know till you try?"

Distractedly she combed both hands through her hair, knowing that she probably wasn't making any sense. She didn't move as he came around the bar and placed his hands on her shoulders. "A few people think I'm not such bad company." His fingers massaged gently.

She cocked her head and eyed him dryly. "Women, you mean."

Dipping his head, he brushed his lips lightly against her temple. "I'm not involved with anyone else, if that's what's bothering you."

She felt her blood stirring to life, her resistance weakening. She fought against it. "It isn't. It's just that I don't want my life complicated."

Wondering why she was so reluctant, he drew away. "Going for golf and lunch with me is a complication?"

"Yes.... No." She let out a long breath. "I don't know."

He knew suddenly that he could pull her into his arms and kiss her into willingness. But it didn't seem fair; for some reason, she had serious doubts about spending time with him. Maybe that guy who had stood her up last week meant more to her than he'd thought. Or perhaps she'd just forgotten how to have fun. He wanted to make the day good for her, to make it easier for her to relax and enjoy. He wound a strand of sable hair around his finger to keep himself from grabbing her and crushing her body against his. "Tell you what. You give it a chance, and if you decide you want to come home in the middle of the golf game, or whenever, we will."

She looked into his eyes. "No arguments?"

He smiled, sensing that she'd already decided to go. "Nary a one."

She relaxed, and he congratulated himself on not moving too quickly and scaring her off. She even returned his smile. "All right. We'll give it a try."

Still smiling, he let his gaze drop to her mouth.

"Your cereal is getting soggy."

He lifted a brow. "So it is."

"I'll get dressed."

"Take your time. I might have a second bowl of cereal."

He watched her leave the kitchen, her lushly rounded hips swaying gently beneath the robe. What he really needed, he thought ruefully, was not more cereal but a cold shower.

Chapter Five

With his hand resting warmly against the small of her back, Quinn guided Kathleen into The Nineteenth Hole. "That wasn't so bad, was it?" They halted to scan the restaurant for an empty table. Saturday was the busiest day of the week at the golf club. The room was filled with weekend golfers, gesturing animatedly, replaying their games.

Kathleen had enjoyed ambling over the course with Quinn more than she would have thought possible. Laughing, she glanced up at him. "Not unless you consider sore feet and sunburn bad."

He rested a fingertip lightly on the end of her nose. His blue eyes were warm. "You *are* a little pink. You should have worn a hat."

The way he was looking at her made her insides quiver. Tossing back her windblown hair, she gave him a chary look. "Thanks a lot. You might have mentioned that three hours ago."

He grinned. "Don't worry. I'll rub lotion all over you when we get back to your place."

Her eyes sparkled with challenge. "Dream on, Gresham."

He studied her with a narrow-lidded look, then bent to plant a quick, hot kiss on her startled lips. "Umm, I will."

For an instant the electric shock of his mouth on hers crackled through her. The contact made her draw a sharp breath. Quinn lifted his head, smiling benignly. "Let's grab that corner table before those two females who are breathing down our necks get there first."

Shocked that Quinn's intimate byplay had been observed, Kathleen half turned to look behind her. The ladies in question returned her gaze avidly. "Er—have a nice game?" she inquired.

"Not as nice as yours, I'll bet," one of the women said with a tolerant smile.

Kathleen giggled as Quinn grabbed her hand and pulled her along with him to the empty table. She was still smothering laughter when Quinn sat down facing her. The two women had their heads together, whispering. One elbow on the bare, shiny tabletop, Kathleen cupped her chin in her hand. "I think you scandalized those women."

He shook his head in denial. "Made their day. All the world loves a lover, even ladies in Bermuda shorts."

She answered his slow, lazy grin with a helpless chuckle. He looked devastatingly male with his wind-disordered hair curling about his chiseled, tanned face. "You think so, do you?"

"Know so." He winked at her and picked up their menus, handing one to her.

She gave him an arch look. "I assume, having played the role often, you've had plenty of opportunity to observe people's reactions."

He grinned. "A gentleman does not discuss his past...ah...indiscretions."

"Hah! Since when?"

He reached for her hand, but she jerked it away. "Does it make you jealous to think of me with other women?"

"Not in the least," she sniffed, and opened her menu. Quinn studied the top of her head. She ignored him and, concentrating on her hollow stomach, began to browse through the entrées. "Mmm, a club sandwich sounds good," she mused.

"The cook makes a great burger." She had become progressively more relaxed as the morning passed, he reflected. Now she was pleasantly tired and wind-blown and had worked up an appetite. It was difficult to remember to keep up your guard in such a state, and he thought that, for an instant there, she *had* been a little jealous. The idea pleased him inordinately. He hid a satisfied smile behind his menu.

"I'll have the burger basket, then." She closed her menu and tucked it back behind the napkin holder. "With everything on it, and the biggest glass of iced tea they've got."

When the harried waitress appeared, Quinn ordered two of everything, surprising Kathleen, since all the other men in the room seemed to be swigging huge mugs of beer. "What, no beer?" Her glance traveled over the room. "I thought it was a club rule."

"I don't drink beer anymore," he told her.

She brought her attention back to him, giving him a concentrated look. "Oh?"

He moved his shoulders and met her eyes. "I drank too much beer once and woke up sick enough to die. Tried to, in fact, but couldn't."

His pointed, penetrating expression made her sure that he remembered the night of his going-away party as well as she did. Was he thinking about it right now? She moved nervously in her chair and clamped down on the thought. That night didn't have to be the only time he'd gotten drunk on beer. Her imagination was running away with itself. "Oh," she murmured. She sat back in her chair, searching for a safer topic of conversation. "I don't know much about golf, but you're obviously quite good. Did you ever think of turning pro?"

He drank from his water glass, then ran a finger over the wet circle left on the table. "No, I'm not that good. Besides, if I did it for a living, I'd have to take it too seriously. I'd rather just horse around with it and have fun."

She remembered that the same carefree attitude had characterized Quinn as a high school athletic. Oddly, it had made him a better player than most of his peers. And his fun-loving outlook had endeared him to the fans. He'd been so different from Patrick, who'd approached every game as though it were a matter of life and death. To Patrick, anything worth doing had been worth doing seriously. As a copter pilot in Vietnam, he'd died while engaged in a voluntary mission, "an undertaking that went above and beyond the call of duty," the letter from his commanding officer had said. Poor Patrick...

She glanced back at Quinn to find him watching her. Not only was he no longer smiling, he looked quite grave. Given the chance, she reflected, she could study his face for hours. The lean, sun-bronzed angles; the mouth that could smile tenderly or become fiercly demanding, depending on his mood. There was intelligence in that face—and something that made her think of a reckless sort of danger. Kathleen sucked in a breath at the thought. She was indeed fanciful today.

"We've established that I play golf for fun," he said quietly. "What do you do?"

Her mind snapped back from its pleasurably sensuous wandering. Get a grip on yourself, Kathleen, she told herself. It wasn't easy to reply in a careless tone, but she did it. "Oh, I read or go to a movie. What I really love is attending the opera."

"The opera?" For some reason, that surprised him. "I make a contribution to the opera guild every year, but I've only been once or twice."

"It's an acquired taste."

"Yes." He was making a mental note to get first-row, center-section tickets for the first performance in the fall.

"Oh, good, here's our food," Kathleen said. "Not a minute too soon. I'm famished!"

They attacked their burgers with healthy appetites. In the middle of the meal, she suddenly exclaimed, "You haven't smoked a cigarette all day!"

He twirled a french fry in ketchup before popping it into his mouth. "I was wondering when you'd notice."

"You quit?"

"A week ago. I got the distinct impression that you find smokers somewhat less than appealing, so I decided to join the ranks of the reformed."

He'd done it to make himself more appealing to her? She couldn't believe it. She felt ridiculously pleased. "Has it been very difficult?"

He considered the question. "Well, I've chewed about a thousand sticks of gum."

She nodded sympathetically. "And eaten a ton of jelly beans?"

"Gum drops," he admitted sheepishly. "I'm considering buying them by the crate."

"It gets easier, and it builds character," she said with a smile, and realized that during the past ten days, when she hadn't seen Quinn, she hadn't been strongly tempted to fall off the wagon. And today, strangely, she hadn't even thought of a cigarette.

"I'll remind myself of that the next time I reach for a smoke," he said ruefully.

His frank admission that quitting wasn't without difficulty made him seem vulnerable, and Kathleen was oddly touched.

They finished the meal with pie and coffee. On the way home they stopped at a garage, where Quinn made arrangements for an employee to deliver and install a battery in his car. "They said it might be a while before they could get to it," he remarked as he returned. He gave her an ingenuous grin. "Guess you'll have to put up with me till they do."

As she drove away, she wondered if he'd told them to take their time, but pushed the thought away as unfair. Anyway, she felt more relaxed with Quinn now. She'd been with him all morning, so what difference could another hour or two make?

She soon discovered that being with Quinn at her house was not the same as being with him on a golf course or in a public restaurant. The moment they entered, she felt herself tensing. She went through the house toward her room, telling him over her shoulder to make himself at home. Standing at the dresser, she brushed her hair and half turned, dropping the straps of her suntop, to examine the extent of the sunburn on her back. Turning around, she found him leaning in the doorway, watching her, and quickly tugged her straps back up.

"Don't mind me," he drawled.

She flushed. "I didn't know you were there."

He straightened, walked over to the dresser and picked up a bottle of body lotion. "Take your straps down again. Lotion should help."

She hesitated, then decided it was silly to make a fuss over such a sensible suggestion. She shrugged partway out of the top again and turned her back to Quinn. When his hand touched the heated skin of her back, she had to bite her lip to keep from flinching. "Sorry, I'll try to go easy," he murmured as he began to apply the lotion with slow, circular movements.

She dropped her head forward and relaxed with a sigh as the light massage continued. She had never imagined a touch so gentle. Soon she was lulled into closing her eyes. Moments later, when she felt a soft, moist pressure at the nape of her neck, it took her a few seconds to realize that the cool and pleasurable sensation was being created by Quinn's lips. She whirled about. "Quinn—"

But that was as far as she got before his mouth stopped her words by closing over hers. Naively, she was unprepared. She had allowed herself to relax and grow unwary under the gentle ministration of his hands, and she wasn't ready for the swift change from solace to passion. The kiss was long and deep, his mouth warm and seeking. She thought fleetingly that he had put down the lotion bottle as he ran both hands slowly over her hips, snugly encased in denim.

His tongue made a thorough, searching invasion of her mouth, and, before she could stop herself, she responded in kind. Reacting to the pull of need, she strained against him, and his arms locked at her waist to draw her closer. She lifted her arms to his shoulders. She could feel the tense flexing of his muscles and the deep throbbing of his heart, and sensed that he was under very tight control.

Her head swam with mingling sensations: easy closeness left over from the day they had shared; the sweet, floral scent of the lotion he had applied to her back; the hard pressure of his body against her; and the hot desire that must have been lying in wait, just below the surface, to spring forth at his demand.

"Quinn," she murmured against his lips. She had to stop him. He had caught her with her defenses down, and if she didn't get control of the situation immediately she was going to give in to the desperate need that streaked through her bloodstream like quicksilver.

Quinn lifted his head, then studied her with eyes that were cloudy with desire. Her face was soft and vulnerable and beautiful. "I want you, Kathleen."

She closed her eyes and tried to find her balance. After a moment she felt her reason returning and stepped back. "No," she whispered, still under the clinging spell of desire. "No, not this time." She blinked, realizing suddenly what she'd said, and turned her back on him. Glancing down she saw that her breasts were half-exposed and tugged the straps back over her shoulders with hands that shook. She placed her hands flat on the dresser to brace herself and stop the shaking.

"Kathleen," he murmured, brushing the hair away from her nape with the back of his hand. He bent, nuzzling his lips into the sensitive curve of her neck. "Ah, Kathleen..."

For a moment she didn't move. When she could, she lifted her eyes to his in the mirror.

"This time," he vowed, "it would be different."

Her blood was beginning to cool. She stared at him, belatedly aware of the inference in his words. Shaking her head, she whirled away from him and walked across the room. All at once her knees were weak. She sat down on the bed and covered her face with her hands.

Quinn knelt before her. He pulled her hands down, holding them in both of his. "I've been trying to tell you all day. Oh, God, Kathleen, I'm sorry for what happened when you were seventeen."

She stared at him, her face ashen. "You were drunk...too drunk to remember."

"I was drunk, but I remember...everything."

Fingers wound together, she pressed her hands against her mouth. Her skin felt cold. She dropped her hands and stared at him, her eyes huge. Then she took a deep breath and made herself say, "I just assumed, when you didn't write, that you didn't remember. But it doesn't matter now. It happened such a long time ago."

Swiftly, Quinn shifted and sat beside her on the bed. "Right now it doesn't seem so long ago." He moved to embrace her, but she stiffened. Frustrated, he let his arms drop and settled for holding one of her hands in his again. "Before I was captured by the Vietcong, I tried to write. Several times. But I couldn't find the right words. I was so ashamed."

"Ashamed... Why?"

His hands gripped hers tightly. "You trusted me... and you cared for me. And you were so young. I took advantage of the situation."

"You were drunk."

He shook his head, refusing to take the excuse. "But I knew what I was doing. I'd been thinking about making love to you all evening, before we went out for that walk. It was entirely my fault, Kathleen."

There was pain in his eyes, and she realized that he'd been blaming himself for years—regretting making love to her. She closed her eyes. "You needn't be so gallant. You didn't force me. I was responsible for my own actions." God knows, she had suffered the consequences.

"I took away your innocence."

She didn't deny it; it was truer than he realized.

"Later, after I escaped from the Cong, so much time had passed...and then I married Mai. After that, I had no right to contact you, Kathleen."

It hurt to hear him speak of the woman he had married. Silence enveloped them for a moment. Sensing him studying her, she opened her eyes. "What are you thinking?" she murmured.

"I'm remembering how sweet you were that night."

Her lids swept down, hiding her eyes and their expression. "Don't."

She looked so fragile sitting there, white-faced, her eyes closed. As if she might shatter at the slightest pressure. "It's difficult to break a fifteen-year-old habit. When I was in prison the memory of you helped me get through the worst times."

"Don't," she said again. Opening her eyes, she took a bracing breath and pulled her hands from his grasp. "I'm going to make coffee."

He watched her leave the bedroom with a feeling of helplessness. She had trusted him fifteen years ago, but a lot had happened since then. She'd grown up, known other men. Maybe one of them had hurt her badly. Whatever had happened to her since she was seventeen, it wasn't going to be easy to get her to trust him again. It might even be impossible after so much time. He went into the kitchen. She was sitting at the breakfast bar, staring out the window. He was sure she heard him enter, but she didn't look at him. The coffee maker's Ready light came on, and he filled two cups, setting hers before her. "I'm sorry, Kathleen," he said finally. "What else can I say?"

He saw the pulse in her throat quiver as she turned her head to look at him. When she spoke, her voice was calm. "Nothing. There's nothing to say. It happened to two other people."

He sipped at his coffee, standing. "The first time I saw Patrick in Vietnam, he told me you'd spent most of your senior year in Florida with an aunt. Did that have anything to do with what happened between us?"

The question shook her composure. She stared at him, trying to decipher what was going on in his mind. He couldn't know about her pregnancy, she told herself; even Patrick hadn't known the real reason she'd been sent to Florida. Her parents had tried to deal with her "condition" by hiding it. Shocked by her pregnancy, and furious because she wouldn't say who the father was, they had banished her to her mother's sister, saying she would have to give the baby away before she could come home. Nervously she drained her cup, then stood and walked a little away from him.

Facing him she asked, "Why would you think that?"

He looked absorbed for a moment, as though he were trying to make sense of something. "I don't know. I guess I felt so guilty over what happened that I turned it into more than it was." He lifted his shoulders and smiled faintly. "My male ego. Sorry."

She relaxed a little. He didn't suspect the truth. "I went to Florida because Dad was very ill and Mother had no time for anything but taking care of him. I thought it would be easier on her if she didn't have anybody else to worry about."

He frowned. "You didn't come back until your father died?"

"A few weeks before." She didn't like to remember that terrible time. A month before she'd gone to Florida, Quinn had been reported missing in action. She had thought him dead, and as her pregnancy progressed she realized that she could more easily tear her heart out than give away his child. After Lauren had been born, she'd refused—in the face of repeated urging from her aunt and ultimatums from her parents—to put the baby up for adoption. She'd begged to be allowed to return home until she graduated from high school. She'd promised that after graduation she would find a job and move, with her daughter, into a place of her own. Her parents had agreed finally, grudgingly. But they hadn't ever forgiven her. They hadn't really wanted her and Lauren; their resentment had been obvious in their every word and look, making sure she understood that she'd ruined their lives. Then her father had suffered a second, fatal heart attack and her mother had blamed Kathleen for that, too. She had broken her father's heart, her mother said. Maybe it was true. She would never know.

Quinn was troubled when he saw her expression shift from wariness to deep sadness. He set down his coffee cup on the bar and moved around to place his hands on her shoulders. "What's wrong, Kathleen?"

She looked up at him, naked pain in her eyes. For a moment she could only shake her head. Finally she breathed, "Nothing, I . . . nothing."

"Don't tell me nothing!" His voice was suddenly harsh, and his fingers tightened on her shoulders. "You look devastated." His face was very close to hers, his breathing strained. Apprehension trembled along her skin. The fear in her eyes finally reached him, and he released her. Dragging one hand through his hair, he swore under his breath. "You don't have to bear it all alone anymore. Talk to me, Kathleen. It might help."

Kathleen stared at him watchfully, hardly aware that she was massaging the spot on her sunburned shoulder that throbbed from his fingers. "It was the worst time of my life," she managed. "I don't want to talk about it."

The anger drained out of him as quickly as it had come. Still hardly more than a child herself, she had been sent from home because having her around was too much trouble. She'd barely returned when she lost her father, and less than two years later, her brother. Of course she didn't want to talk about it. He tucked a wayward strand of hair behind her ear. "Forgive me. I'm an insensitive clod." He laid a light kiss on her temple.

His quick tenderness was almost her undoing. She drew a sharp breath that burned her throat as she struggled against crying out. "Hold me," she begged. "Just for a minute."

He reached for her, and she wound her arms around his neck and clung. She pressed her face into his shoulder. She was trembling. He didn't know what was going on in her mind at that moment. He knew only that she needed comfort, as a frightened child needs comfort. He held her and stroked her. "It's all right, honey. It's all right."

After a few moments she looked up at him, her eyes misty with unshed tears. She swallowed convulsively and, without thinking, he kissed her trembling lips. She responded immediately. Her lips parted in unconscious invitation, and he framed her face with his hands and deepened the kiss. The kiss grew hotter and moister, and she swayed against him.

His fingers caressed her face, and Kathleen could feel the fire building inside her. But when she realized what was happening, the fire went out. It would be easy to rekindle it, she knew. She had only to let Quinn go on kissing her and close her mind to everything but physical sensation. But there was too much pain between her and Quinn. No amount of physical pleasure could change that. She had let her emotions rule her when she was seventeen, and Quinn had left her with a baby and married somebody else. If Mai had lived, she would be with him now, and he wouldn't be in Kathleen's house.

Quinn felt her go still in his arms. She wasn't clinging any longer, but simply leaning against him as if all passion had been drained out of her. He released her lips and tilted her face up to his. Her eyes were full of pain. "Are you all right?"

Her irises were glittery and opaque as she stared at him. She made a soft, gulping sound and straightened, as though waking. She sighed, a weary, defeated sound. "Yes."

The silence that surrounded them was thick with unuttered thoughts. The sound of the doorbell made them both jump. "It's probably the man with my battery," Quinn said. "I'll go."

"Quinn," she said as he reached the kitchen door, "would you lock the door when you leave? I think I'll lie down for a while. I'll call you when I know anything about Van."

She could not have made her position clearer. She didn't want to see him again, except in regard to his son. Quinn left, feeling totally frustrated. As soon as he could get to a store, he told himself grimly, he was going to buy a pack of cigarettes.

An hour later, Quinn was back home. By the time he'd reached the store he'd had time to reconsider and had purchased a large sack of gumdrops instead of cigarettes. Now he roamed his house like a caged animal, occasionally stuffing another piece of candy into his mouth.

He had thought of little but Kathleen for the past hour. For a while that morning she'd almost been the vivacious Kathleen he remembered. But as soon as they'd reached her place, she'd reverted as quickly as any chameleon ever changed colors. As he thought about it, he became more certain that what had happened to her in the past fifteen years had affected her even more deeply than he'd thought. Losing her father and Patrick had been difficult for her, naturally, but she should have been able to deal with it by now. He reached for another gum drop. There was much more; he felt it in his gut.

While he'd been in the Vietcong prison he'd thought about Kathleen almost constantly. He'd imagined her dating many young men, falling in and out of love. He'd pictured the girl he'd watched grow up finishing high school and going to college, a popular, carefree coed, her future an array of opportunities. It had seemed important that she be living such a life. He'd assumed she would marry before he saw her again. He wondered why she hadn't.

He'd known for months she was living in Oklahoma City but, until he had proof to the contrary, he'd considered himself a married man. He had been sorely tempted to try to see her anyway, but his sense of fair play had finally won out. When he'd learned Mai was dead, the first thing he'd thought of was finding an excuse to contact Kathleen.

He sighed heavily as he wandered aimlessly through his bedroom and back into the hall. Well, he'd contacted her, all right, and she was so changed. What— or who—had destroyed the happy-go-lucky girl he'd known?

The Kathleen he remembered would have gotten married by now. If there had ever been a girl made for marriage and a family, it was Kathleen Kerns. He kept coming back to that.

In the end there seemed only one logical conclusion he could come to. Sometime during the past fifteen years she'd had a disastrous love affair. Some man had broken her heart so totally that she hadn't allowed herself to love again.

Some other man had taken her sweet, unselfish love, used it until he wanted somebody else, then discarded it and Kathleen, like leftovers thrown on a trash heap. Some other man . . .

It outraged him to think of how it must have been, but it was the only reasonable explanation for the guarded woman Kathleen was now.

Chapter Six

You're not very talkative this evening," Maggie remarked as she and Kathleen left the dinner table and carried their sherbet to Maggie's living room. Kathleen had supplied the chops and vegetables for the meal, Maggie the salad and dessert.

Kathleen went to her usual place in the corner of Maggie's blue Victorian sofa, kicking off her shoes as she settled in. "I'm a little tired." She spooned raspberry sherbet into her mouth.

"Busy today, huh?"

Kathleen shot her friend a penetrating look. Maggie was watching her with a thoughtful expression. "I was on the golf course all morning."

Maggie savored a bite of sherbet before she said, "With that good-looking man I saw leaving your place this afternoon?"

So she'd seen Quinn. Maggie's studiedly careless tone made Kathleen uncomfortable. "Yes."

"I didn't know you played golf."

"I don't. I went along for the walk. Do you know how far it is around a golf course?"

"Umm, I used to play with Dink sometimes. I took lessons and everything, but I was never very good. My heart wasn't in it. I never could see much point in knocking a little white ball around."

"My sentiments exactly." Kathleen applied herself to her dessert, hoping Maggie would let the subject drop. But Maggie wasn't about to.

"Was that good-looking fellow the one from your past? Quinn, isn't that his name?"

Kathleen sighed. "Yes, that was Quinn. How did you know?"

Maggie smiled. "Because you've seemed troubled all evening, like you were last week when you told me about him."

Kathleen shook her head. "I'm not troubled...."

"Absorbed, then," Maggie amended, but she thought she'd been right the first time. Quinn's sudden reappearance had thrown Kathleen into confusion. "And who could blame you? He's really something." The few men Maggie had seen going into Kathleen's side of the duplex during the past year had never come more than twice. Whenever she'd mentioned them to her friend, Kathleen had shrugged, plainly not deeply interested in any of them. Her reaction to this man from her past was different, though. She couldn't shrug him off as easily as she had the others. Kathleen might find it disturbing, but Maggie was encouraged. She wanted Kathleen to have somebody to share her life with.

"He's something, all right—something I don't need in my life right now." Or ever, Kathleen added to herself, intent on collecting the last of her melted sherbet.

"That shouldn't be a problem."

"What do you mean?"

"You've managed to get rid of several suitors since I've known you. Why should this one be any different?"

Kathleen frowned. "Quinn isn't a suitor, exactly."

"What exactly is he?" Maggie's expression was too innocent to be real.

"An old friend," Kathleen responded after a pause.

More than that, Maggie suspected, but she knew better than to say it.

"Only..." Kathleen continued, then gestured helplessly. "I can't explain it. It's too involved."

"May I give you a piece of advice?"

"Sure, why not?"

"Don't shut the door on this man until you're sure you no longer feel anything for him. Will you at least think about it?"

Kathleen was taken aback by Maggie's words. She didn't want to give Maggie the impression that she cared for Quinn—even though it was true. After fifteen years she still loved him. It was stupid and hopelessly romantic of her, but there it was. She shook off her troubling thoughts. "I'll think about it. Now, can we talk about something else? Have you heard from Bert since you got home?"

Maggie ducked her head. "He called me this week. He's going to be in town next weekend and wanted to know if we could get together."

"You've known this for days, and you're just now getting around to mentioning it?"

Maggie looked embarrassed. "It's no big deal, Kathleen. Bert and I simply like each other's company."

"He's coming here especially to see you, isn't he?"

"Well, he didn't say that...."

"Wonderful." Kathleen laughed. "A smart lady once told me not to close the door on a man until I was sure I didn't feel anything for him."

"Okay, okay." Maggie smiled sheepishly. "I get the point."

Jeb Drewly called from Washington on Thursday morning. "Kathleen, the congressman has been in touch with his contact at the Australian embassy in Saigon. They've done some checking, and it seems that investigator's report is accurate. The boy, Van

Thieu, isn't in school. He works long hours in the rice paddies.''

"How can the grandparents get away with that?" Kathleen asked indignantly.

"Underdeveloped countries don't have the same priorities that we do," Jeb said dryly. "Education takes a back seat when people's major concern is getting enough food to survive."

"That poor child." She knew that Jeb was right, but the unfairness of it had never struck her so forcibly before. It was difficult to accept that the sheer accident of where a child was born so often sealed his fate.

"There are millions of them, Kathleen."

"I know," she murmured, "but we can't do anything about millions, can we? Maybe we can do something about one little boy, though." To think she had called Quinn selfish for wanting to get Van out of there.

"Depends on how receptive Gresham is to extortion."

"Of course," Kathleen said sarcastically. "That's politics, right? When all else fails, grease a few bureaucratic palms."

"That too. But I think we can satisfy the Vietnamese officials with a few thousand dollars total. It's the grandparents who are going to be the problem."

"The Australian contact talked to them?"

"Yeah. At first they flatly refused to consider turning the boy over to his father. They said they need him to work in the fields. After several conversations they told the Australians they would let Van go for thirty thousand American dollars.''

"They're his grandparents, for heaven's sake!" Kathleen exploded. "You'd think they'd be grateful that Van has an opportunity for a better life. Don't they have any feelings for him at all?"

"They're poor, Kathleen. I'm not talking about welfare poor, like we have in this country. They're peasants, and they'll starve if they don't have enough food to last until the next growing season.''

"But thirty thousand!"

"That's their asking price. They'll expect to negotiate. If we handle them right, they'll probably take ten. Say fifteen, with what we'll need for the government officials. Will Gresham pay it?"

"I'll have to ask him." She was sure she knew the answer, but she couldn't speak for Quinn.

"If he wants us to go ahead with the negotiations, tell him he'll have to sign an affidavit that he's the boy's father and will accept full responsibility for his care and support.''

"All right. I'll get back to you, Jeb." Kathleen hung up and dialed Quinn's office. His secretary informed her that Quinn had flown to London on business Monday morning, but was expected back the next day. "When you speak to him," Kathleen said, "will you ask him to contact Congressman Smythe's office? He'll know what it's about."

Kathleen replaced the receiver. She was, she realized, disappointed at not being able to give Quinn the message immediately. Or was it more than that? Had Jeb's call given her pride the excuse she needed to talk to Quinn, which she'd wanted to do all week? It was difficult to sort out her motives where Quinn was concerned, so she didn't even try.

She expected to hear from him all day Friday, but he didn't call. He was probably somewhere over the Atlantic and hadn't checked in with his office before he'd left London. Chances were she wouldn't hear from him until Monday.

A Buick with Kansas license plates was parked in Maggie's driveway when Kathleen got home at six-thirty. Bert has arrived, she thought with a smile as she let herself into her side of the duplex.

Several times during the evening she wondered how Maggie and Bert were getting along next door. She heard Bert's car leaving about ten-thirty that night and hoped Maggie would call to let her know how things had gone. But Maggie didn't. Finally, at eleven, Kathleen got ready for bed.

She had been propped up in bed, reading a mystery novel, for half an hour when her doorbell chimed. Some sixth sense told her it was Quinn even before she'd put on her robe, switched on the porch light and opened the door. He was wearing a brown business suit and looked drawn and tired.

"Hi." There was a quick flare of warmth in the navy depths of his eyes. "I called my secretary when I changed planes in New York. She gave me your message."

She drew her robe closer across her breasts, then jammed her hands into its deep pockets. "You look beat. You didn't have to come here straight from the airport. It could have waited until Monday." Dear heaven, it was good to see him again. Had it really been only a week?

He looked at her steadily, the porch bulb highlighting the prominent angles of his face. "I didn't want to wait. I'm sorry if I woke you."

"No, you didn't." Naturally he couldn't wait to hear what she'd learned about his son. She'd spoken without thinking, because his unexpected presence was making her nervous and unsure.

"May I come in?"

She realized that a part of her was reluctant to give up the barrier of the screen door between them. She felt as exposed as though she stood before him naked. Did he have any idea how glad she was to see him? "I'm sorry. Come in."

"You've heard something about Van?" he asked as he closed the door behind him.

Kathleen turned and settled on the arm of the couch. She waved her hand toward a chair, but Quinn remained standing, his hands in the pockets of his rumpled brown trousers, waiting for her reply.

"Oh, Quinn, that poor boy." Kathleen looked up at him with eyes darkened by compassion. "Everything your investigator told you is true. They send him to the fields every day like—like a dumb beast. He would have been better off left in the orphanage."

"Maybe," he muttered. In a gesture of exhaustion he took his hands from his pockets and rubbed them over his face. A faint sandy stubble shadowed his cheeks. "It's probably a case of which is the lesser of two evils." As though he were suddenly too tired to stand, he shrugged out of his jacket and loosened his tie, tossing them aside, and dropped down on the couch beside her. Her arm was resting along the back of the couch, and he let his head fall back against it as he looked up at her.

"The orphanage would definitely have been better," she told him. "Someone from the Australian embassy went to see the grandparents. Do you know what they said?"

"They want money," he said tonelessly. It wasn't a question.

He'd closed his eyes, and she watched the play of emotion on his face. He was fighting not to release his anger and frustration. It would solve nothing. Mai's parents were a fact of life that he had to deal with, as he would a troublesome hitch in a business deal. Indignation would only complicate the issue.

"How did you know?"

"It follows. That's the kind of people they are, or maybe just the kind of world they live in." He opened his eyes and gave her a thin smile. "This is the only chance they're ever likely to have for a windfall. It's asking too much to expect them not to take advantage of it."

"That's what Jeb Drewly said." Quinn's blue eyes were bleak, and she wanted to comfort him, but she wasn't sure how.

"How much do they want?"

"Thirty thousand, but Jeb said they'd probably settle for ten. And another five for the Vietnamese officials involved."

He let out a long, weary breath. "It could have been worse. Evidently they haven't guessed how much I'm worth. I'll pay it, of course. The thirty thousand, if they won't come down. Have Drewly tell the negotiator to use his own judgment. I want it finished, the quicker the better."

It must be cutting him up inside to think of the cruelties his son had suffered. Without thinking, she placed her free hand on his cheek and drew his head against her. "They want an affidavit, too, saying you're Van's father and will pay his traveling expenses and provide a home for him."

"I'll do it first thing Monday and send a messenger to your office with it. Anything else?" He turned his face into the soft side of her breast, and the delightful smell of soap and feminine fragrance filled his nostrils. He had thought about her all week; missing her had been a dull pain in his body, needing her a heavy ache in his groin.

"No." His breath was seeping through her robe to warm her breast. Neither of them moved for long moments. His nearness was like a salve to her spirit. She didn't move for fear of breaking the spell. All week she had been telling herself that she would confine her relationship with Quinn to business; it was the only safe course to follow. It had been easy to see the logic in her reasoning while Quinn wasn't with her and she could be objective. But she had no objectivity at this moment, only too many regrets and a tangle of other feelings that she couldn't unravel. "What did you do in London?"

The words were soft and low, but they indicated to Quinn that, though they had exhausted the news about Van, she was willing to let him stay for a while. He put his arms around her and pulled her down off the arm of the couch into his lap. When she stiffened, he drew her gently to him and tucked her head beneath his jaw. He only wanted to hold her for a bit, he told himself.

"It was a buying trip. I found a few things that will retail profitably through the stores, but no great bargains." He could have added that the excitement of tracking down and haggling over bargains hadn't been there this trip; he had been more interested in getting back home and seeing her again. The message she had left with his secretary had provided all the reason he needed to come here directly. He was tempted in the closeness of that moment to tell her the whole story about Van and Mai. Telling would ease his mind, but it would also put her in a compromising position with the congressman. It was not, he realized, the time to involve her further in his problems. If that time ever came it would be after he had Van safely with him.

Wordlessly he gathered her close. Her arms curved around his neck, but he sensed a tentativeness in the embrace. Caution, he told himself. But he discovered that he wanted her more than he ever had before. Not just the softness of her body against his, the taste of her mouth, the physical joining. He wanted to get inside her psyche, to share her deepest thoughts and emotions as if they were his own. He wanted both to be a part of what she was and her to be a part of him in a deeper sense than the merely physical. He wanted no more barriers between them. Tenderness spread through him, and he stroked her hair with exquisite gentleness. Something of what he was feeling must have been communicated to her, for she lifted her head and looked at him with a question in her eyes.

His eyes were full of things she couldn't read. He'd never looked at her exactly that way before. What was he feeling? Then his lips touched hers.

The kiss began with reverence. That was the only word that could adequately describe it, Kathleen thought dimly. Quinn's lips were as soft as down on hers, moving only with the greatest care, as though this were the first time he had ever kissed her, as though he were afraid of hurting her. Or as though the very act of kissing were new and strange to him. She was deeply moved, and returned his kiss with equal care.

He felt her relaxing in his arms. The taste of her lips, as they softened and parted under his, was like the nectar of the sweetest flower. He framed her face with his hands, his touch as gentle as though he held fragile crystal. Slowly he deepened the kiss.

Kathleen felt her tightly reined emotions unfolding, like petals reaching for the sun. She pushed her fingers into his hair and let her tongue dip into the pleasures of his mouth. He groaned and lowered her to lie on her back on the couch, taking the kiss deeper all the while. Kathleen held his head between her hands, not wanting him to lift it, not wanting him ever to stop kissing her in this magical way.

Unnoticed, her robe had fallen open. With a shaking hand, Quinn slipped the narrow straps of her gown off her shoulders and freed her breasts. They fell into his hands, soft, feminine treasures, their tips hardening as he brushed them with his thumbs. Quinn's heart was pumping so furiously that his breathing was ragged and labored. He had never felt so overwhelmed by emotion as he did in that moment. No other woman had ever had such a powerful effect on him.

He lowered his head to nuzzle her breasts, to take the aroused tips into his wet mouth one by one and stroke them with his tongue. Kathleen was riding a rising tide of pleasure, her mind a hazy fog incapable of connected thoughts. She was aware only that an overload of sensation had swamped logic. Uttering soft sounds of pleasure, she moved beneath Quinn. She had never wanted anything as much as she wanted to make love with Quinn, to forget everything but the rightness no other man had ever made her feel. Her fingers dug into the muscled flesh of his arms, and his name sighed from between her parted lips.

For a moment Quinn tried to clear his head. He had meant to use caution, but his body was throbbing, his desire demanding release. "Kath ... oh, Kath ..." He didn't even know he had spoken.

Kathleen heard. The name he had called her as a young girl—murmured in the same throaty tone as on the night he had first made love to her—penetrated the hypnotic fog of feeling. Suddenly she was seventeen again, lying on a grassy bank overlooking a lake, and Quinn was the adored, almost mythical being she loved more than the rest of the world combined. The passion drained out of her. With a faint, but tortured, sound she became instantly still and unresponsive in his arms. She didn't even know she was crying until Quinn lifted his head and asked, "Kathleen? What's wrong?"

She was crying for the romantic girl she had been and for her baby, the baby Quinn had never known. She was crying for Quinn, too. But she couldn't articulate her feelings. Some sorrows were too deep for words.

Unable to speak, she shook her head.

"Did I hurt you?"

There were many answers to that question, but she knew he meant just now. Again she shook her head. Her face was the picture of tragedy. The raw pain in her eyes frightened him. Baffled, he sat up and gently rearranged her gown to cover her breasts. What had he done? Why wouldn't she talk to him? She continued to look up at him without moving.

He didn't want to leave her this way, but he sensed that he wouldn't be able to reach her if he stayed. She had gone somewhere inside herself, and he couldn't follow. He fought against a sinking feeling that he might never be able to reach her again. It was a cruel irony that at the very moment when she was farthest away from him, he could admit to himself that his feelings for Kathleen were far deeper than physical attraction. He loved her; perhaps he always had.

Shaken, he reached for his coat and tie. "Are you all right?"

"Yes," she whispered, even while her heart knew it to be a lie. With a tremendous effort she almost managed to smile.

He stood for a moment in silence, feeling unaccountably awkward. "Well, I'll go, then."

She nodded, and he walked to the door and let himself out. Kathleen still didn't move for several minutes after she heard him drive away. Finally she sat up and pulled her robe about her. Driven by the same compulsion that periodically took control of her, she went to the bedroom and opened a bottom drawer of the dresser. Burrowing beneath stacks of lacy undergarments, her fingers found the smooth face of the photograph. She drew it out and, staring at it, lowered herself to sit on the side of the bed.

Lauren had been six weeks old when the picture had been taken, a precious bundle of plump, pink flesh.

Her hair was thick and jet-black. People had said it was baby hair and would fall out as permanent hair grew in, but Kathleen hadn't had Lauren with her long enough to find out if that was true. Lauren's bright-blue eyes stared out of the photograph in an expression of surprise caused by the camera's flash. It was the only picture of her baby that she had kept. Every time she fell prey to the compulsion to take it from its hiding place and pore over it, she told herself that she should get rid of it. But she couldn't make herself do it.

Lauren wore a lace-trimmed pink dress that Kathleen had made before the baby was born. She'd had a strong feeling from the start that she would have a girl. With her finger she traced the pattern of the ruffled lace along the hem of the dress and around the tiny Peter Pan collar, remembering the love and care that had gone into the garment.

"I love you, Lauren," she whispered.

She continued to run her fingers over the glossy image—the tiny dimpled hands, rosy cheeks and button nose—until tears filled her eyes faster than she could blink them away. With a sudden, racking sob she clutched the photograph to her breast and wept until she had no tears left.

Chapter Seven

Monday a messenger delivered the affidavit to Kathleen's office. In spite of what Quinn had said, Kathleen had expected him to deliver it in person. She had spent the weekend repairing her defenses to face him. Now she would have a little more time to get over what had happened Friday night.

She dismissed the messenger and wandered to her office window. She felt the inward loosening of tension that comes when a dreaded confrontation doesn't materialize. At the same time she felt an unreasonable disappointment that Quinn hadn't come himself. She didn't understand herself. She'd had the opportunity to become more deeply involved with Quinn Friday night and had decided against it. Difficult as that had been, it was the right decision. She wasn't regretting it now, was she?

Opening the envelope, she took out the signed affidavit and read:

By this affidavit the undersigned, Quinn David Gresham, a resident of the town of Oklahoma City in the state of Oklahoma, U.S.A., does solemnly state and affirm that he is the true and legal father of Van Thieu, a male Amerasian born 23 March, 1974, in Saigon, South Vietnam, who lived in the Saigon Orphanage from April, 1974, to September, 1984, when he went to reside at the home of his maternal grandparents in Cu Chi, South Vietnam. The said Quinn David Gresham does also state and affirm that he was legally married to Van Thieu's mother, Mai Van Minh, on September 2, 1973, the ceremony being performed by a United States military chaplain (copy of marriage license enclosed herewith). The said Quinn David Gresham does further state and affirm that he wishes, and does hereby request, that his son be permitted to live permanently with him in the United States and promises to pay all expenses involved in Van Thieu's immigration and to provide Van Thieu with a home and proper education. The said Quinn David Gresham hereby solemnly swears that he has the desire and financial means fully to support his son until such time as Van Thieu reaches his majority and is prepared by education and other necessary means to support himself.

It took but an instant's calculation to realize that Mai had already been pregnant when Quinn married her. But that didn't change anything. Quinn *had* married her, probably had waded through a formidable skein of red tape to do so. He certainly wouldn't have done it unless he'd loved her. It always came back to that.

Kathleen must never forget that after he'd made love to her fifteen years ago, he'd fallen in love with and married another woman. Illogically, Quinn's affidavit had made the situation more real than it had seemed before. Kathleen shivered when she remembered how close she had come to letting Quinn make love to her. She had to keep reminding herself how it had turned out the first time she'd done so, how it had nearly destroyed her, how long it had taken her to get over it and go on with her life.

For a moment that night she had even come close to telling Quinn everything. Thank goodness she hadn't. The past was dead. What good would it do to tell him now? It would only open all her old wounds again. As for Quinn, he was too involved in getting his son back to have room in his heart for a tiny daughter he had never known.

Kathleen returned the affidavit to its envelope and dialed the congressman's Washington office. "Jeb," she said when the aide came on the line, "I'm sending

Mr. Gresham's affidavit to you by express mail. He has agreed to pay the grandparents whatever they demand in exchange for his son."

"Good," Drewly said. "I've been in touch with Immigration, and it looks as though it's simply a matter of getting all the required forms to the right people. You can tell Gresham that once we've struck a deal with the grandparents there will be no other major obstacles in our path."

When she hung up, she stared at the phone, knowing she had to call Quinn immediately. Bracing herself for the ordeal, she dialed.

"Mr. Gresham isn't in the office right now," the secretary told her. "May I take a message?"

"This is Kathleen Kerns." She hesitated. "When do you expect him back?"

"I'm not sure he'll be back at all today."

She couldn't give the message to the secretary. It was too personal. "Never mind then. I'll call back tomorrow."

Maggie was working in her backyard when Kathleen got home from work. Kathleen changed into her jeans and went out to weed her garden and talk to Maggie through the chain link fence that separated their two yards.

"Did you get rested up from your big weekend?" Kathleen greeted the older woman.

Maggie had been so absorbed in clipping shubbery that she hadn't heard Kathleen come outside. She jumped at the sound of Kathleen's voice and whirled around. "Gracious, if you were a snake, you'd have bitten me. I didn't know you'd come home."

"Just now." Kathleen squatted and began to pull weeds from the rock garden. With the arrival of May the daffodils and tulips had given way to irises, eight varieties of them in colors ranging from deep purple to rust. "Well?"

"Well, what?" Maggie inquired innocently.

"You heard me. I want to hear about your weekend."

"Oh, is that what that subtle hint meant?"

They laughed, and Kathleen stopped her weeding to study Maggie. "It was a success."

Maggie blushed prettily. "How can you tell?"

Kathleen cocked her head. "You look—oh, I don't know. Refreshed, content, something like that."

Maggie's flush deepened. "You're teasing me."

"No, I'm not." Kathleen decided not to mention the fact that she'd noticed Bert's car parked in Maggie's driveway all Sunday night. It had still been there when she'd left for work that morning.

"All right," Maggie relented, "I did have a good time."

"And Bert?"

Chuckling, Maggie bent over a holly bush to wield her clippers. "I guess he did, too. He wants to come back next weekend. I told him I'd think about it and let him know."

Kathleen sat back on her heels to admire the clump of white irises she'd finished weeding. "What's to think about, if you enjoyed the weekend so much?"

Maggie straightened, her expression grave all at once. "I'm afraid things are moving too fast, Kathleen. I don't want to make a serious mistake at this time of my life. Bert's lonely and—well, I guess I am, too. I want to give us both time to be sure of what we're doing."

She's falling in love, Kathleen realized suddenly. She never imagined it could happen to her again, and it scares her. Maybe she believes she doesn't deserve another happy relationship, that if she cares too much she'll get hurt. Well, Kathleen knew about that kind of caution.

"I'm sure Bert will understand if you put him off this weekend."

Maggie was still frowning thoughtfully. "What do you think I should do?"

Kathleen laughed. "I'm hardly the person to give you that kind of advice. Do whatever you want to."

"The problem is, I'm not sure what that is."

"Oh, I think you are," Kathleen told her. "You just have to give yourself permission."

Maggie's face cleared, and she smiled. "I guess you're right. Women probably make these things too complicated."

Kathleen thought about that remark of Maggie's when Quinn phoned that night. In spite of her assurances to herself that she'd been right in deciding not to become more involved with him, the sound of his voice sent a thrill of gladness through her. Maggie had no idea what real complications were, Kathleen reflected. Her feelings about Quinn—now, that was complicated!

To cover her confusion she launched immediately into a word-for-word account of Jeb Drewly's phone call that morning. "I tried to reach you today, but your secretary didn't know if you'd be coming back to the office. I was going to call you tomorrow."

"My secretary could have reached me if you'd told her it was urgent." His irritated tone held a challenge.

"I didn't think a few hours would matter. Aren't you happy about what Jeb said?"

"Sure, but I expected that. Right now I'm more concerned about what happened Friday night. I've been trying to figure it out ever since."

"It's a woman's prerogative to change her mind."

"Don't be flip, Kathleen," he returned, and Kathleen recognized the impatience in his voice.

"Apparently you've had a bad day. Maybe we ought to hang up now and try this again later."

"Why are you afraid to talk to me?" he threw back. "You used to follow me around, talking. Why can't we talk that way anymore?"

"Oh, Quinn..."

"Just listen to me for a minute, okay? I want it to be the way it used to be between us."

"That was a long time ago. I was a child then. Now I'm an adult."

"I'm not buying that any longer, Kathleen." He ground out the words. "There's something very wrong; you've put up barriers against me. I don't know why, but I'm going to find out. I want to see you. Tonight. Now."

She didn't even have to think about it. She felt too vulnerable to cope with Quinn tonight. "No."

"Damn it, Kathleen!"

"Goodbye, Quinn. Maybe we'll talk later, when you can be more reasonable." Her hand shook uncontrollably as she replaced the receiver.

On his end, Quinn slammed the phone down with another oath. Devil take the woman. Why was he pursuing her when she so obviously wanted nothing to do with him? He had an address book full of phone numbers he could call to provide himself with the company of a charming woman for the evening. He thought about a few of them briefly, but he didn't go in search of his little black book. He didn't want to be with any of the others.

His mind still on Kathleen, he fished a crumpled pack of cigarettes and a lighter from a drawer. He'd already lit a cigarette when he realized what he was doing. Cursing, he crushed it out and tossed it and the crumpled pack into the wastebasket. He'd been through the worst time, the first two weeks after he quit smoking; he'd be damned if he'd let Kathleen make him fall back now.

He was too restless to stay in the house. The driving range at the club was lighted until ten at night.

He'd go out there and kill a bucket of balls; maybe he'd get some of his frustration out that way.

Saturday morning Kathleen stood at her kitchen window and watched Maggie and Bert playing badminton in Maggie's backyard. They were laughing like a couple of teenagers. Bert was a stocky man of medium height with a full head of thick, silver hair. Kathleen felt sure he'd look more at home in a business suit than in the striped shorts and white T-shirt he now wore. Maggie was obviously enjoying herself this weekend as much as she had a week earlier. Kathleen smiled, wondering what Jeff and Ellen thought about the blossoming romance they were responsible for initiating. Had they really expected their parents to hit it off so well?

Maggie glanced up and saw Kathleen at the window. "Come out here and meet Bert," she called.

Kathleen went into the yard and walked over to lean on the fence. Maggie's face was rosy from the exertion of the game; at the same time she looked, in her white shirt and shorts, as though she'd just stepped out of a bandbox.

"Bert, this is my landlady, Kathleen Kerns. Kathleen meet Bert Clawson."

Kathleen shook Bert's hand across the fence. "It's good to meet you, Bert. You two are making me feel guilty about sitting in the house and not taking advantage of this beautiful day."

"Yes, the weather's perfect, isn't it?" Bert commented.

"Would you like to join us?" Maggie asked.

"No, thanks. I think I'll walk over to the park."

As Kathleen went back inside, she heard Bert say, "What an attractive young woman. She doesn't seem very content, though."

And Maggie replied. "Man trouble."

You don't know the half of it, Maggie, Kathleen thought as she closed her door.

Kathleen heard Maggie and Bert laughing again as she left the house, having changed into shorts, a shirt and canvas walking shoes. She hadn't seen Maggie so carefree in the entire year she'd known her. Love is grand, she reflected as she walked briskly toward the neighborhood park—or hell. There didn't seem to be anything in between.

It was safer never to give your heart, but a life without someone to share it could end up being prison. She tossed back her hair, hoping to rid herself of such uneasy thoughts. Lord, she was morbid today. She knew why she was feeling so restless. Her telephone conversation with Quinn Monday evening had ended unsatisfactorily, and she hadn't heard from him since. He was merely obeying her wishes by leaving her alone, but perversely that didn't please her. Maybe Maggie had been right in telling her not to shut the door on Quinn. But at this point Kathleen was so confused she didn't know what was best.

Several children were playing on the jungle gym and swings in the park, and Kathleen found an empty bench beneath a spreading oak tree from which to watch them.

A young mother wheeled a baby back and forth across the grass in a canvas stroller and cautioned two little boys who were climbing and swinging over the jungle gym like monkeys. The baby, a girl, judging from its pink sunsuit and bonnet, was asleep. Dark ringlets peeked out from beneath her bonnet, and one dimpled fist rested against a chubby cheek. As Kathleen watched, the baby stirred and blew a bubble from her mouth. Her eyelids fluttered open, and two deep blue eyes stared at Kathleen.

Kathleen wasn't one to coo over every baby she saw, but she suspected this one could turn her heart to mush, given half a chance. The baby's mother bent over the stroller, obstructing Kathleen's view. She looked away, swallowing the lump in her throat. The baby reminded her of Lauren. Kathleen closed her eyes. Lauren would have been fourteen now, and, for a moment, Kathleen tried to picture her daughter grown into a teenager. How would Lauren have looked at fourteen? Like Kathleen—or Quinn? Both of them, or neither of them? When she opened her eyes, the young mother had called her sons down from the jungle gym and was pushing the stroller across the grass away from Kathleen.

Restlessly, Kathleen stood and followed one of the park's winding paths. This outing is supposed to take your mind off morbid thoughts, she reminded herself. Get with it.

She had stopped to admire the park's rose garden when a deep male voice called her name. Turning, she saw Quinn striding toward her. He wore cotton cord trousers and a wine-colored vee-necked knit shirt. Foolishly, Kathleen's heart flipped over.

"How did you know where to find me?" she asked when he reached her.

"Your renter told me where you'd gone."

"Oh," she said inanely. Looking into his blue eyes, she became aware that she was smiling. "Well, I haven't heard anything else about Van."

"That isn't why I'm here." The fact was, he realized as he passed a frustrated hand through his hair, that he wasn't quite sure why he was there. He'd awakened that morning with the knowledge that he had to see her, but now that he was with her he felt like a teenager asking for his first date. Come to think of it, he'd never felt such a lack of confidence as Kathleen made him feel lately, even as an adolescent. He let out a long breath. "Let's walk."

After a slight hesitation she nodded and stepped back on the path. He strolled beside her, his hands stuffed into his trouser pockets.

"So, why are you here?" She was looking up at him, her brown eyes curious.

Why indeed? he wondered. If she made him so uncomfortable, why wasn't he with some other woman, trying to get Kathleen out of his system? Because he didn't need some other woman. He needed Kathleen.

"I wanted to see you," he said, and took her hand. "Is that a crime?"

She laced her fingers through his, and the thrill of his touch ran up her arm. "No," she murmured, "it's not a crime."

At her response Quinn felt his tension slowly receding. She seemed almost glad to see him. Maybe it hadn't been a mistake to come after all. "Your renter and her husband were getting ready to go somewhere. They asked me to tell you to collect their mail in case they didn't get back tonight."

"That's not her husband; it's her boyfriend."

He let out a sound of surprise. "Really?"

"Really. Their children are married to each other, and they fixed them up. Maggie and Bert met, and I guess rockets went off. Anyway, he's been here the past two weekends. They woke me up this morning playing badminton in the backyard."

"Badminton? You're kidding."

"I thought it was kind of cute."

"Hmm. That's nice. Everybody needs somebody."

She shot him a look, but he continued to stroll, his expression as nonthreatening as an expression could be. Had he meant something personal by that last remark? After several moments of silence she said, "I'm sorry for being so short with you Monday night. Sometimes I don't know how to take you, Quinn."

He laughed. "Join the club."

She smiled. "You too? I thought I was always pretty straightforward."

He halted to look down at her. "You are the least straightforward woman I know. You're keeping secrets, and I don't know how to get you to share them with me."

"Some secrets are better left hidden," she said gravely.

He drew her across the grass to a bench, sat her down and sprawled beside her, his arm draped loosely around her back. "How are we going to improve this relationship if one of us is hiding things?"

Her eyebrows rose. "I wasn't aware that we have a relationship."

Quinn caught her chin in his fingers and turned her face toward him. He looked deeply into her soft brown eyes. "I think you're very much aware of it," he said quietly. "At least, you feel something between us when we're together. Why else would you be so defensive with me?"

There was no point in denying the obvious. She sighed and shrugged helplessly, diverting her look from his. He leaned over to give her a brief kiss before he grinned and said, "You can relax. We can't do anything but talk out here in broad daylight with all these people around."

She returned his smile after a moment and settled comfortably into the crook of his arm. "When Van comes to live with you, what will you do with him when you're away on business?"

"I hadn't thought about it much. I'll have to find somebody to stay with him."

"It's going to be different, being responsible for an eleven-year-old boy. Especially at first. He'll probably need a tutor until he gets integrated in school. Can he even speak English?"

"I don't know. I've learned not to borrow problems. I'll just take it one day at a time." He stroked her arm idly and looked distant for an instant. "I got very good at that in the prison camp."

She gazed at some children playing tag about a hundred yards away. "Did they give you that scar on your cheek, the Vietcong?"

He never talked about his imprisonment, tried never to think about it. And he didn't want to talk about it with Kathleen. But he remembered how he'd accused her of keeping secrets and forced himself to answer. "Yes. They were interrogating me, and I was refusing to answer their questions. One of them had a whip, and he laid my cheek open with it."

She looked stricken. "I'm sorry."

"It's all right." Surprisingly, it wasn't as hard to talk to her about it as he'd feared. "I preferred the whip to some of their other methods. One of their favorite games was to hold a gun on you and give you meaningless commands. Stand straight! Look at me! Put your hands up! Sometimes they made us keep our hands up for an hour at a time. You got so you didn't much care whether they pulled the trigger."

Impulsively, she put her arms around him in a gesture of comfort and rested her head on his shoulder. "How were you captured?"

"We were flying our wounded out of a combat zone in the Ia Drang Valley. Our troops had pulled back behind a hill, and our commanding officer sent three helicopters back for the wounded. Then they let loose with mortars. I had a soldier slung over my shoulder, and I tried to make it back to my helicopter with him. For several minutes I couldn't see or hear anything. I wasn't sure I was running in the right direction. Evidently I wasn't because when my ears stopped ringing and the firing died down enough for me to hear the Hueys revving up, they sounded farther away than I'd thought. The helicopters took off, and the VC swarmed out of the bush and took me and the soldier I was carrying captive. He'd passed out by that time, and he died the next day."

"Your crew left without you?" Kathleen asked indignantly.

"If they hadn't, we'd all have been killed. Before long I wished I had been." The words weren't a bid for sympathy, but a raw statement of fact.

"I don't know how you survived two years as a prisoner."

"I learned to disassociate. I stayed inside my head most of the time." He stroked her hair. "You were there with me."

She didn't think the admission had been calculated to melt her heart, but it did. She couldn't think what to say. Finally she asked, "How did you manage to escape?"

"The VC were retreating, dragging about a dozen prisoners along with them. We were weak from lack of exercise and food by then, and every time we stumbled they'd hold a gun to our heads and threaten to blow our brains out. Finally I decided I'd rather be shot than go on like that. About the time I was deciding that, some American copters spotted us and began to fire. In the panic and confusion I ran into the brush and kept going until I dropped. Two days later I crawled into a Seventh Cavalry camp. I didn't know much after that until I woke up in a hospital well behind the lines. When I recuperated, I went back to Saigon and looked up Patrick." He glanced down at her quickly. "Well, you know the rest."

No, there were countless things she didn't know. "How long after that was Patrick killed?"

"Two months."

"He was evacuating wounded?"

"No, he was on search and destroy. His copter was shot down. He'd been flying for days and was due for a rest, but he kept volunteering. He seemed obsessed." His arm tightened around her. "If he had to die, Kathleen, it was the best way. It was over for him in an instant."

After a long silence she whispered, "I'm glad you told me, Quinn."

"You're the only person I've ever talked to about it. Thank you for letting me." He continued to stroke her hair gently, wanting to keep the closeness that had developed between them during the past few minutes.

Kathleen sat up and looked at him with stricken eyes. "I'd give anything to be able to wipe out the past fifteen years. Life is so cruel."

"Not all of it. Come on," he said tenderly. "I'll drive you home." He kept his arm around her as they left the park.

Chapter Eight

A tray of cheese, crackers and fruit, with a bottle of wine, sufficed for lunch. Quinn found a golf tournament on television, but kept the sound low. They set the food on the coffee table and made themselves comfortable with throw pillows on the living-room floor.

Kathleen had kicked off her shoes and sat, cross-legged, with her back against the sofa. Quinn half reclined beside her, his head resting on a stack of pillows. When they had arrived at her house, it had seemed natural to invite him in. Then it turned out to be noon, and she couldn't send him away without lunch. Now he seemed to have settled in for the afternoon.

Quinn turned away from the television screen to refill their wineglasses. He noted the way she sat, her back straight and her hands clasping her knees; the position seemed self-protective. "You're very pensive."

Kathleen couldn't seem to shake off the lingering undercurrent of melancholy that had been engendered when Quinn talked about his imprisonment and Patrick's death. She voiced the thought that had been troubling her. "You said Patrick kept volunteering for missions, that he seemed obsessed. That doesn't sound like Patrick. He wasn't impulsive; he thought things through." Indeed, in their school days, Quinn had been the impulsive one. Patrick's role had often been to put on the damper when Quinn's enthusiasm burned too hot.

He sat up and lifted his hands to her shoulders to massage them gently. "Vietnam changed a lot of things, Kathleen. You don't live in hell without being affected by it."

"But to deliberately keep going back into hell, when you could have a respite. . . ." She shook her head uncomprehendingly.

"As long as he was moving, doing something," he said softly, "he didn't have to think about anything else."

She let out a long, weary breath. "You mean, like being sent home maimed—or not coming home at all?"

He clamped down on a need to tell her the complete truth. With an effort he said only, "Yes."

"Or," she went on musingly, gazing through the atrium doors at the sunny, summer idyll of her patio and flower garden, "coming home and knowing you'd be so changed that nothing would be the same. Home would be spoiled for you."

He handed her a wineglass. "Patrick wouldn't want us to mourn for him the rest of our lives." He lifted his glass. "To the present—and the future."

She studied him over the rim of her glass, thinking suddenly that he was holding something back. Protecting her from too much insight into what Vietnam had done to the men who fought there. She touched her glass to his and sipped her wine. "It can't be easy for you to forget that time."

He set down his glass and bent to brush first one of her cheeks, then the other, with his lips. "I don't want to forget everything. I'll always remember you."

She laughed shakily. "I wasn't there."

"Yes, you were." He ran his hands gently up and down her arms.

She felt the weakness creeping into her and made herself disregard it. "Oh, I know you said you thought about me sometimes when you were in prison."

"Fantasized." He took an earlobe between his thumb and forefinger and tugged it gently. "This— you and me together like this—it's almost eerie how close it is to the way I used to fantasize it. Food and wine, a long, lazy afternoon..." His hand left her ear to lift her hand slowly to his lips. "You touching me." He lifted his head to gaze musingly at her hand, then placed the hand, fingers spread, against his chest.

She could feel the deep, steady beat of his heart through his knit shirt. She sucked in her breath. "You must have fantasized about a lot of girls."

He heard the uncertain timbre of her voice and smiled. "No, only you. Honestly." He laid his finger against her bottom lip and pressed lightly to expose the moist tip of her tongue. She knew he was thinking about kissing her, and a quick thrill ran through her. "I relived every second of that night beside the lake," he said gravely. "Again and again." His blue eyes held hers. "I knew it shouldn't have happened, and I felt guilty about taking advantage of you, but it was a memory I treasured, too. For your sake, I was sorry it had happened; for mine, I was enormously grateful. God, you were so wonderful I sometimes thought it couldn't really have been the way I remembered, that I must have dreamed it."

Feeling desire flutter through her, Kathleen stared at him. He was mesmerizing her. The burning intensity of his eyes and the seductively languid tone of his words were making her feel dizzy. She had forgotten she was still holding her glass until she spilled wine on her jeans. It brought her partially back to her senses. Blinking, she drained the glass and set it back on the tray. Then she rose and strode to the atrium doors where she stood with her back to Quinn.

"Kathleen..."

Still she didn't look at him. "You had too much beer that night to remember the way it was. You took the reality and built it into something romantic and grand."

She heard him getting up. He walked over and stood behind her, his hands resting on her shoulders. "No, I remember everything that happened. Exactly." His fingers toyed with a smooth strand of hair that fell over her ear. "I wanted you so much that night I thought I'd go crazy."

His voice was rough with feeling. Turning around, she looked up at him and shook her head. "I'm not that girl anymore. I can hardly remember her."

"I know," he said softly. Watching her, he rubbed his thumb along her collarbone and over the creamy column of her neck. "Neither of us is the same. We'd be prime examples of arrested development if we were."

She cocked her head and took a deep, bracing breath. "Well, then—"

"Let me finish." His hands curved around her neck to draw her closer. "The man I am now still wants the woman you are. More than ever." He brushed his lips lightly over her mouth. "Such a lovely mouth," he whispered.

She tilted her head back slightly, trying to steady her senses, but he followed and deepened the kiss. Finally he lifted his head to mutter unsteadily, "Delicious, too. I could go on kissing you for hours."

"Could you really?" she asked with a low laugh. "I have another idea. Let's finish the wine and see if sanity doesn't return."

He followed her to the couch, watching silently as she poured out the rest of the wine and handed him his glass. Then he put his arm around her and pulled her close to his side. With a half-smile that seemed to say he was relishing a secret, he emptied his glass, then disposed of it. She smiled at him, sipped and brought her glass to his lips. "Want to share?"

His hand closed over hers on the stem, and he felt the faint tremor in her fingers. "Kathleen." His voice was low as he tilted the glass and drained the small amount of wine that remained. Impatiently he set the glass aside, then cupped his hand around her neck to drag her closer. His mouth on hers was hard and questing. "If this is insanity," he growled, "I don't ever want to be sane again."

Kathleen shifted to put more distance between them. Think what you're doing, she cautioned herself with a rush of panic, what's going to happen if you don't fight this treacherous weakness. She was so confused. She didn't know what she wanted at that moment. She needed more time to be sure. "It's the wine," she murmured. She could feel the tension in him, in the tightening of his hand at her waist, and she knew that they were very close to the edge of danger. She tried to blink away the unfocused haze that clouded her vision, but it wouldn't go. The only thing she could see clearly was Quinn's face, the seductive sensuality of his lips, the way the color of his eyes deepened with wanting her. She spread her fingers over his chest. "I'm afraid I'm about to make a terrible mistake," she admitted.

His expressive eyes held none of the doubt that she was feeling. He knew now that she wanted him as much as he wanted her, but he had to make her realize that for herself. He fought back his pounding need. Brushing back her hair with both hands, he planted soft kisses along her hairline. Then he kissed her eyelids closed before he allowed himself another delectable taste of her mouth. She smelled of sunshine and the sweet, honeysuckle fragrance of cologne. Her scent seduced him and threatened to destroy the final restraints on his passion. He struggled to hold on, and, after a long moment, he lifted his head. He could see her pulse throbbing madly in the hollow at the base of her throat.

She dragged her eyelids open slowly; the effort was almost too much for her. "Quinn..." she murmured uncertainly, her mind clouded, her senses swamped in the liquid depths of desire.

Her shuddering, indrawn breath seemed to be a part of his own heartbeat. He wanted to crush her to him, to plunder her sweetness and tear away her remaining doubts. But he restrained himself. Let her take the lead, he ordered himself as he fought his throbbing passion.

"I can't think," she murmured, more than a touch of wonder in the words. "I—oh, Quinn..." Suddenly she plunged her fingers into his hair and pulled his mouth back down to hers. I'm never going to get enough of this, was all she could think. Never.

He groaned deep in his throat as his arms tightened around her convulsively. His blood raced, thick and hot, like molten lava in his veins, and passion was a whirlpool, sucking him down. He battled the compulsion to give up and let go. Let her be sure, he warned himself. And, oh, God, let her hurry.

Her mouth on his was seeking, hungry. They were prone on the couch when she broke the kiss long enough to mutter, "There's not enough room here...the floor is better."

Quinn grasped the full meaning of her words and the last thread of control snapped. Somehow he got to his feet, lifted her and laid her in the nest of pillows on the floor. As he bent over her, her hands clutched him greedily and her mouth fused with his. In the heavy, dreamy afternoon stillness their mouths fed on each other ravenously. The only sound was their labored breathing.

Restlessly her hands tugged at his shirt. The time it was he who broke the kiss so that he could pull the shirt over his head. With a dreamy satisfied smile she stroked her hands over the smooth, muscled flesh of his back and blazed a trail of wet open-mouthed kisses along his neck and shoulder. With a ragged, oxygen-starved breath, Quinn clasped her head and held her still while his mouth plundered hers.

In the brief moments between deep, delirious kisses he dealt fumblingly with buttons and snaps, stripped himself and pulled her clothing from her soft, glowing flesh. He had dreamed about this moment for so many years. And it was even more agonizing than he had dreamed. If he could have, he would have loved her slowly, gently, drawing it out and savoring every nuance, but he was incapable of restraint. When at last she lay naked beneath him, he looked at her through a haze of urgent need and thought his laboring heart would explode in his chest.

She was more than he had remembered or ever imagined. Her taste was more intoxicating than the finest champagne. The loveliness of her body—the perfect breasts, the slim waist and softly flaring hips, the long slender legs—literally crushed the breath from his lungs. With a gasp that was as much pain as pleasure, he covered her mouth with his and took her in a rough, primitive frenzy that was all wildness and storm, consuming him and sweeping away finesse and gentleness.

Swept into the tempest with him, Kathleen lost herself in the raging onslaught. Clinging to him, she matched the turbulent tempo of his lovemaking until the world was distilled to nothing but Quinn's mouth ravishing hers and his hard, lean body moving over hers, pushing her higher and higher toward the pinnacle. Then, in a blinding flash of heat and sensation, they reached the apex and plunged over.

Splintered into a million fragments, drained, moist with perspiration and dazed in the aftermath, Kathleen felt herself slowly coalescing again. She became aware of Quinn's weight on her, of his gasping as he buried his face in her hair. With arms that felt weighted she held him and closed her eyes against the hot stinging dryness that she knew would be a deluge if she allowed it to turn into tears.

Quinn was too spent to move. His limbs quivered with the sudden relaxation of tension, and he dragged air into his lungs in deep gulps. Slowly coherence returned. Something had happened to him that had never happened before. His body had been taken over by a part of himself that had broken through for the first time—something dark and primordial. Dismayed, he tried to remember how it had happened. They had been sitting on the couch and suddenly she had become the aggressor, her kisses eager and demanding. Until then he'd managed to retain a semblance of control, but the change in her had shattered that. He remembered lifting her and laying her on the floor, undressing her.... After that everything was lost in a madness to possess her. And somehow in the possessing, he had become the possessed. It had happened so quickly, and he had felt absolutely driven.

Like a man staggering away from a cyclone, he was dazed, full comprehension still in abeyance as he dealt with small details. He must have handled her roughly. Oh, God, had he hurt her? He lifted his head, which still felt too heavy for his neck to support, and looked down at her. Her lashes were dark against the rosy flush of her cheeks. Her hair was tangled, her breath still coming a little too quickly from between soft, love-bruised lips. She was incredibly beautiful, with that special glow that a woman had only after lovemaking. For an instant he felt the madness stir to life in him again. He closed his eyes and clamped down on the feeling ruthlessly. When he felt in control, he opened his eyes and asked huskily, "Kath, did I hurt you?"

Without opening her eyes she sighed softly and let her hand trail over the moist skin of his back. She was only just realizing what had happened herself. She didn't want to move too quickly and destroy the wonder that was still washing through her. She smiled faintly as she thought of the contrast between Quinn's wild, demanding passion and the vulnerability in the hoarse question he'd just asked. Still smiling, she opened her eyes. His were now almost black with concern and uncertainty. Tenderness welled up in her, and she stroked his shoulder gently. He had stripped her soul naked, and she didn't think it would be possible to rebuild her defenses against him. She didn't know yet what she was going to do about that.

"No," she said, and laid her hand against his cheek, "you didn't hurt me."

She saw gratitude flood into his eyes. He feathered kisses over her face. When he lifted his head again he seemed to have come to grips with something.

"I love you, Kath. I think I always have."

Her eyes narrowed, grew solemn. "You don't have to promise undying devotion because we made love," she murmured.

"Don't," he said curtly, but the touch of his warm lips on hers was light and gentle.

"Don't what?"

"Don't be offhand about this. I'm in love with you, and I want you to know it."

She sighed and turned her face into his shoulder. "If you say so."

He grasped her chin and forced her to look at him. "I do say so. Kath, once you loved me, too. I know you did. Can you love me again?"

She responded with the utmost gravity. "You'll have to give me some time to think about it. Love involves promises for the future. I'm not sure I believe in the future anymore."

Frowning, Quinn removed his weight from her, although he continued to shelter her in his arms. His lips moved against her forehead as he spoke. "What do you believe in, then?"

She was silent for a long moment, thinking. "Myself, I guess. I know I can depend on me."

"And nobody else?"

"I can't answer that now. Maybe in the fullness of time..." Sitting up, she smiled tentatively. "Would you like to stay for dinner?"

"Yes." His eyes answered her smile.

"Can you grill steaks?"

"I'm practically a pro at it. I always fix them when I entertain at home. It's hard to ruin a good steak."

Absentmindedly she combed her hair away from her face with her fingers. "Do you entertain often?"

"Hardly at all lately. But grilling steaks is like riding a bike. You never forget how."

She chuckled and rose to her feet gracefully. As she began to dress, she said, "You watch the end of the golf tournament while I go to the supermarket."

"You sure you don't want me to come with you?"

She shook her head. "I need to be alone just now."

Don't come too close, she was saying; give me some space. He tried not to be hurt by her retreat. She went into her bedroom; while she was gone, he dressed. When she came out with a handbag slung over her shoulder, he kissed her and said lightly, "I'll check out the grill. See you later, love."

She drove up and down streets that she hardly saw, absorbing what had happened with Quinn.

He loved her, he said, but what did the word mean to him? Mere sexual attraction? Enjoying being with a woman when he wanted her there and forgetting about her when he didn't? Or did it mean more? Commitment? Forever?

She had believed he loved her long ago, and he had left her. He had always loved her, he'd said. Well, she'd always loved him, too, and look where it had landed her. She sighed, wishing it were possible to see into the future. But life gave no guarantees. You took it one day at a time, with no promises for tomorrow.

And maybe that wasn't all bad. Maybe the uncertainty of the future taught you to have faith in other people without taking them for granted. And it taught you to appreciate the good times while you had them.

When she finally reached the supermarket she felt more at peace with what had happened.

When she returned to Quinn, almost two hours later, he bit his tongue to stop himself asking where she'd been besides the grocery store. Surely it hadn't taken two hours to purchase the small bag of groceries she had. Maybe she'd just parked somewhere to think. Whatever she had thought about, she had apparently settled it in her mind. She seemed more relaxed as she made coffee for them, then mixed a blackberry cobbler and slid it in the oven. They took their coffee into the living room.

She nestled easily against him on the couch. "Did the golf tournament turn out the way you expected?"

"Trevino came back to win," he told her. "I like that. Proves it's never too late for a determined man."

"Hmm. I presume you're not talking about golf."

He traced a fingertip over her chin, enjoying the healthy glow beneath the faint tan of her skin. "Correct."

"I'm not sure I agree with you," she mused, laughing when his finger stilled. "I mean, at some point it's too late for everybody."

"While there's life, there's hope."

Leaning over, Kathleen picked up her coffee cup and cradled it in both hands. "Not necessarily. There will be a time when even Lee Trevino can't win the PGA, no matter how determined he is. Another example. Women can't have babies after they've gone through menopause, no matter how much they'd like to. I could go on...."

With a wry smile he watched her drink, then set her cup down again. When she settled back against his shoulder, he kissed her languidly. Afterward her eyes were darkly liquid. "Why did you mention having babies?" He tucked her hair behind her ear and nuzzled her neck.

She struggled to keep her thought processes intact as his warm breath feathered the sensitive skin behind her ear. "It merely came into my mind as an example." To steady herself she cupped her hand against the back of his head and shivered involuntarily as his teeth nipped her earlobe.

"Which means it was in your subconscious all the time." Carefully he outlined her jaw with silken kisses, and for a moment she lost her train of thought completely. "Interesting."

"What is?" she murmured, because she'd forgotten what they were talking about.

He slid farther down on the couch and took her with him. Lying on his side, he settled her against him and kissed her before he replied. "The thought of having a baby was in your subconscious before you said anything about it."

"Wait a minute." She shook her head to try to get her thoughts in line. "I didn't say anything about having a baby myself. I was speaking hypothetically."

He knew better than to push her too far. "I stand corrected." His lips began to roam her face, and she lost track of time. "You know," he said finally, "I've always thought you had a strong maternal instinct."

"Quinn, I thought we'd covered that." Somehow his hand had found its way beneath her shirt and was stroking her midriff.

"I'm on a new track now."

She caught his wandering hand and held it still. "I think I know where it's going, too."

He laughed softly. "I was thinking about Van."

"Oh?"

"I'm going to need help with him, Kath. Will you help me?" He felt her stiffen, and raised his head.

She looked at him with something in her eyes that shocked him, because it looked like helplessness and a touch of fear. "I can't, Quinn."

"Sweetheart, I know you have your own life, your job. I'm not asking you to be a full-time mother."

She shook her head. "You don't understand. I can't love another child—" There was an even deeper fear in her eyes as she halted abruptly, sucked in her breath and lifted her fingers to her lips, as though to hold back more words. He noticed that her hand was shaking.

"Another child?"

"You're confusing me. I didn't mean that the way it came out. I meant I can't get involved in your life with your son." She smiled then; it was a seductive smile, if a little forced. And she moved against him so that her breast pressed against his hand.

Quinn sighed helplessly. He would try to figure out what she'd said later. Right now he couldn't focus on anything but the way her body was so pliant against him, the weight of her breast on the back of his hand. He turned his hand over and cupped the soft mound, and her nipple hardened instantly beneath his palm. "I can't seem to concentrate on Van right now, anyway."

"I know what you mean." She felt drunk, her eyes heavy as they tried to focus on him. As his hand stroked her breast, she felt her whole body melting. "You didn't start the charcoal yet, did you?" Restlessly, she arched her body, moving her breast under his hand.

"No." Quinn lifted her shirt to expose her breasts. He bent to suckle, and Kathleen moaned.

"I'm glad," she murmured mindlessly, "because I want you to make love to me—for a long, long time."

Even while her mind tried to reconstruct its defenses, her body couldn't help surrendering to him. This time, he thought, as his tongue and lips continued to explore and savor her breasts, he would love her slowly, sweetly, completely.

"Quinn..." She said his name like an urgent plea, and her fingers plunged into his hair.

He rose and lifted her into his arms. Her arms clung about his neck, and her face as she looked up at him was aglow. I'll make her love me, Quinn vowed. I'll make myself so necessary to her that she'll have to love me. And then he couldn't think at all. He covered her mouth with his and carried her slowly, blindly, into the bedroom.

Chapter Nine

Dappled sunlight fell on Quinn's face. He mumbled something in his sleep, and his arm, which lay heavily on Kathleen's waist, twitched. She shifted to her side. Earlier they'd packed a Sunday picnic of fried chicken, potato salad and baked beans. They'd followed an old highway out of the city and through the suburbs until they reached the sparsely settled countryside. After another hour of idle driving they'd found the perfect picnic spot, a spreading oak tree beside a stream in a meadow at the end of a little-traveled dirt road. The farmhouse over the hill, they'd noticed, was abandoned. The pastureland obviously belonged to an absentee owner. Since they saw no cattle, they ventured through the barbed wire fence.

Technically they were trespassing, but there was little chance of anyone seeing them. No other car had come down the dirt road since their arrival.

They had eaten their fill before stretching out on the quilt to nap, loosely entwined in each other's arms. The previous night Quinn had finally gone home after extracting her promise to spend Sunday with him. For Kathleen the weekend had become an unfocused dreamscape against which she and Quinn laughed, talked, ate and made love. She didn't even want to think about Monday and the intrusion of the workaday world.

After picking up their litter and repacking what was left of the food, she had fallen asleep next to Quinn, but his restless movements had awakened her after a half hour. She had lain there, content to gaze into the leaves overhead and listen to his deep, even breathing. Now she rested her cheek on her bent arm and watched him.

He looked younger when he was sleeping, more like the boy she had known fifteen years ago. It was the first time she'd had the luxury of looking at him to her heart's content without his being aware of it. She lay quite still, not wanting to wake him.

His sandy hair lay in rumpled curls on his forehead. His thick, light-colored lashes rested against tanned skin stretched taut over prominent cheekbones. His nose was straight, with the barest suggestion of a hump at its bridge. His lips were finely sculpted, the lower fuller than the upper, above which glistened a few tiny beads of moisture.

In the past two days this man, so defenseless in sleep, had become Kathleen's lover, and perhaps it was natural that she found him beautiful to look upon. She longed to touch his face, and it was difficult to keep her hand still at her side. As though he sensed her steady perusal, even in his sleep, he mumbled an incoherent protest and flopped over on his back, flinging one arm across his forehead. His eyelids fluttered and, frowning, he continued to move restlessly. Kathleen sat up, wondering whether she should wake him. As she hesitated, he began to thrash about on the quilt.

"No..." he muttered, and then more fiercely, "No!"

"Quinn." She placed her hand on his shoulder and shook him gently.

His head rolled from side to side. "Get away from me!" He threw his arms out, and Kathleen ducked just in time to avoid being hit. Still asleep, his face was contorted in what must have been horror.

She bent over and shook him harder. "Quinn, wake up."

He flinched as though her touch had burned him, and ground his teeth. "I told you—stay away from me!" Arms churning in a swimming motion, he struggled to a sitting position. Only then did his eyes come open. For an instant he stared at Kathleen with an expression of undiluted pain.

She lifted her hand to stroke his cheek. "It's all right. You were dreaming." She saw the pain recede as comprehension came into his eyes. He groaned, shook his head and passed his hands over his face.

He shuddered. "God, it was so real."

She brushed the tangled blond hair off his forehead. "Were you dreaming about the prison camp?"

He stared at her for a long, measuring moment, then nodded.

She had an urge to enfold him in her arms like a child, but his reluctance to admit that he'd been dreaming about the camp made her hold back. "Does it happen often?"

He got to his feet abruptly. "Not as often as it used to." He lifted the picnic basket and, when she stood, folded the quilt and tucked it under his arm. Picking up the basket, he said, "Let's head back."

In the car she ventured, "Talking about it might help."

He started the engine. "No, it won't."

He kept his eyes on the road as he drove. She gazed at his profile, noting the stubborn set of his chin. "Quinn, it's not an admission of weakness to talk about things that trouble you."

"Leave it, Kathleen. We've talked about it enough. This has been a great weekend. Let's not spoil it now."

She sighed helplessly, laid her head back against the seat and closed her eyes. Male pride, she thought irritably. Why did men think that if they ignored a problem it would go away? Obviously Quinn's Vietnam experience was still very real to him. He hadn't been able to put the imprisonment behind him. She wondered if he still dreamed about Mai, too, about the brief, tenuous existence they had shared amidst the chaos of war before she and their son were swept away from him. Would Kathleen ever be able to question him about that? And if she did, would he talk to her about Mai?

During most of the drive back to Kathleen's house they were silent, each sunk into the privacy of their thoughts. When they were inside Quinn reached for her and pulled her against him. His arms tightened around her. "I didn't mean to snap at you. I'm sorry."

She hugged him. "It's all right."

He brought his lips down to hers. The kiss was full of a throat-aching poignancy that neither of them could put into words. Within seconds they were both trembling with desire.

"The more I make love to you," Quinn muttered thickly, "the more I want you. It's like an addiction."

She smiled softly. "Fortunately there aren't any serious side effects. You can't OD"

He chuckled and swept her into his arms. "Thank God for that." He strode into her bedroom and laid her gently on the bed. Muted sunlight filtered through the cracks in the slatted window blinds. Bending over her, he began to unbutton her blouse. "I want to see if your body is really as beautiful as I remember."

She lay quiescent as he undressed her slowly. His hands lingered reverently on her skin, caressing and adoring. Her lashes fluttered down, and with a deep sigh she gave herself up to the pleasure of his touch. "Umm," she murmured, "nice."

His hands stroked her shoulders and brushed her nipples tantalizingly before molding themselves to the undersides of her breasts. Kathleen stretched languidly, moaning as she felt her blood heating.

His lips whispered over her breasts and stomach, his breath warm and moist on her skin. His fingers stroked her legs, working their way with exquisite slowness toward her inner thighs.

"Kath," he murmured as she sighed and moved restlessly. Whispering her name over and over, he slid his hand between her legs, stoking the embers in her blood to full flame. "Tell me what you want."

"You know..." His mouth silenced her sweetly. Slowly his fingers found her moist core. "Quinn..." And then her breath caught as he lowered himself over her and his mouth tasted again of her mouth.

All the while his fingers continued their slow relentless stroking, and she groaned and began to move with the rhythm. "That's it," he whispered against her lips. "Show me what you want, love."

Dazedly she realized that he was naked, too. Her hands wandered over his smooth, firm flesh with a mindless need to touch him everywhere. Surely no man had ever loved a woman like this, she thought wonderingly as he moved his lips leisurely over her face and throat and breasts. As she felt her own need growing, then clamoring for release, a part of her mind could marvel at the unhurried pace he set. Again and again he brought her to the edge, only to ease her back once more as he savored the taste of her mouth and skin and soothed her with murmured approval.

Her senses responded greedily, drinking in every word and touch, every nuance of feeling. Sinking deeper into the pleasures he was orchestrating with such lazy care, she stifled the impulsive desire to plunge into the final explosion of passion. Banking her own need, she sought to give him equal pleasure. She moved her body against his in the way that she knew he liked. She let her hands roam freely over him. Their murmured pleasure and whispered requests added to the arousal wrought by their hands and mouths.

Never had she received, nor needed to give, such tenderness. She wanted only to please him, to make him feel as loved and desirable as she did. She wanted the lovely sensations they were sharing to go on and on. Her body had never been more alive, more aware in every pore. The pleasure was so exquisite that it had to press closer and closer to the point of no return.

Their breathing quickened; the movement of their hands accelerated. Quinn relished the scent of her, the lingering remnant of country air and sunshine. Her faintly perspiring skin was warm and silken smooth as his hands skimmed over it from one delight to another. His appetite for the taste of her was insatiable. Her taut nipples had a dark, feminine flavor that almost drove him mad. The damp skin of her shoulder was faintly salty. Her mouth contained an endless supply of sweetness. He returned again and again to its nectar, toying with her tongue, nipping her lips.

A shudder ran through her, and her fingers clenched in his hair. Her heavy-lidded eyes were bottomless wells of need as she arched her body in mute pleading. He slid slowly into the hot, moist welcome of her body, and caught her gasp of response in his hungry mouth. Fighting the wild and clamoring demands of his body, he set a slow, savoring pace that tested the limits of his control. As the rhythm of their lovemaking slowly increased he whispered words of love and praise without knowing fully what he said.

Kathleen trembled beneath him, her body attuned to his slightest touch, like the quivering strings of a fine violin. She moaned as she reached the crest, and still he held himself in check, bringing her to the peak once more. Again and again he fought back his rising passion until every muscle in his body shivered involuntarily with the effort.

Helpless, she clung to him and murmured his name repeatedly, like a mantra. He had succeeded at last in demolishing her every barrier and restraint; she was totally his, her mind filled with him, her body weak from the pleasures of his lovemaking. He couldn't hold back any longer. With a mighty surge he buried himself in her and let his passion break free.

The fire roared out of control and consumed them.

A long time later awareness returned. The capability for coherent thought trickled back and was soon lost in drowsiness. Spent, they slept deeply, and this time there were no troubled dreams for either of them.

The sun had gone down when Kathleen awakened. Dusk had filled the room with soft shadows. Smiling at the memory of their lovemaking, Kathleen slid toward the side of the bed.

Quinn's hand reached for her. "Where are you going?" he asked sleepily.

"To take a shower."

He yawned and stretched, then propped his head on his hand as he watched her disappear into the bathroom, a look of contentment on his face.

Kathleen stood under the warm spray, her head thrown back, her eyes closed. It felt wonderful. She groped for the bar of soap, found it and slowly lathered her body, turning slowly beneath the pelting stream of water. After shampooing and rinsing her hair she stepped from the stall and reached for a fluffy white towel.

She dried her body, then toweled her hair. Standing in front of the foggy mirror, pulling a comb through the damp strands, she realized that she'd forgotten to bring any clothes into the bathroom with her. She cracked the door and said, "Quinn, would you mind handing me my blue kimono? It's in the bottom right-hand dresser drawer."

Quinn pulled on his briefs and opened the drawer. His hand fell on slick-surfaced paper. He took it out and switched on the lamp on the dresser. It was a photograph of a baby. A confusion of questions sped through Quinn's mind as he stared at the photograph. He discarded most of them. There was no writing on the back of the picture. The child probably belonged to a friend of Kathleen's, he decided finally.

"Quinn, where's my kimono?"

He rummaged in the drawer and came up with a royal-blue silk garment, undoubtedly the kimono, and thrust it around the bathroom door. Still studying the photograph, he sat down on the side of the bed. It was a beautiful baby. Dark hair, and bright, intelligent eyes. In the bathroom Kathleen turned on the hair dryer. Quinn continued to ponder his find. Unaccountably, he sensed that he'd stumbled onto a secret.

Why did Kathleen keep the photograph hidden away in a dresser drawer? It had been on top of a stack of nightclothes, so she must have had it out recently. Why? He attempted to recall what Kathleen had said yesterday, something about not being able to love another child. Another. The word's connotations hadn't really registered until now. He tried to shake off an odd feeling of apprehension.

A few minutes later Kathleen came out of the bathroom. "I feel so refreshed—" She broke off abruptly, staring at the photograph that Quinn held out to her. "What are you doing with that?" She snatched it from his hand. "You have no right to go through my things!"

Quinn's apprehension increased. Her reaction was too defensive. "I didn't go through your things. It was on top of your kimono."

She tried to recover. Turning her back abruptly, she slid the picture into a dresser drawer. When she turned around she had regained some of her composure. "I don't know what made me say that. I guess it was the surprise. I'm sorry."

But Quinn wasn't fooled. He had seen the color drain from her face, seen the panic in her eyes. The skin around her mouth was still ashen, and her smile was brittle. He stood up slowly. "Whose baby is it, Kathleen?"

She walked to the nightstand, picked up her wrist-watch and put it on. Her movements were too studied, and she wouldn't look at him. "Friends. You wouldn't know them."

The tension in the room was so taut that it crackled. "Maybe I would. Who are they?"

She waited a few seconds before she faced him, too long for her response to have been spontaneous. "Why this sudden interest in the child of strangers?" She smiled too brightly. "Are we running out of things to talk about so soon?" Without waiting for a reply she headed for the door.

Quinn took three long strides and blocked the exit. "Who are they, these friends?"

"This is ridiculous." She stuffed her hands into the pockets of her kimono. "Aren't you going to get dressed?"

He was close enough now to see the pulse beating rapidly at the base of her throat. "Why don't you want to talk about that baby?"

She stared up at him for a long moment, her dark eyes stricken, vulnerable. The fragile facade of carelessness crumpled. She bent her head and covered her face with her hands. "Give me a break, Quinn, please." The words, muffled by her fingers, were nakedly pleading.

He couldn't let the subject go. He placed his hands on her shoulders. Her muscles were rigid with tension. He massaged gently. "Kath," he said quietly, "tell me."

For a moment she didn't move or respond. In the street a car passed, its driver accelerating suddenly, making the tires squeal as he took the corner. The sound seemed totally foreign in the oppressive silence of the bedroom. Kathleen lifted her head. "It's Lauren." Her voice cracked, and she clutched her throat.

He waited, but she only looked at him, her face drawn. "Lauren?" he prompted.

She closed her eyes, drew in a deep breath. "My baby." There. She'd said it. What happened now?

Perhaps he should have known. Her every word and gesture since she'd seen the picture had indicated the depth of her trauma. But he hadn't been prepared for the words, for their starkness. For a moment he was sure he'd misunderstood, but the words reverberated in his brain, and he realized that he hadn't. Her shoulders sagged as she watched him take in her meaning. He enfolded her in his arms. He buried his face in the fragrant cloud of her hair; it smelled of the lilac-scented shampoo she'd used. "Kath..." he muttered. "Oh, my God, Kath."

She clung to him fiercely, and he could feel her struggling not to cry.

His eyes burned. After a few moments he asked gently, "Where is she now?"

She swallowed with difficulty. "She died." He lifted his head to look at her, but she pressed her face deeper into the crook of his neck. "It hurts too much to talk about it. Just don't let go of me, please." She'd used up her courage; she couldn't tell him that Lauren was his. Not now.

Quinn held her, rocking her gently back and forth, murmuring comforting words and stroking her back. Gradually she stopped trembling, but she continued to cling to him tightly. It gave Quinn several minutes to deal with his shock.

It wasn't the time to ask any of the questions that were clamoring in his head, chief among them: Who was the baby's father? Jealousy stabbed through him. God, it almost killed him to think of another man fathering Kathleen's child. Had Kathleen been married to him? Had the baby's death been the catalyst for a divorce? Or had he gotten Kathleen pregnant with an illegitimate child, then washed his hands of her? If he'd done that Quinn would enjoy strangling him. He would have to know the whole story eventually, but she was too upset to talk about it now. Maybe later she would tell him of her own volition.

It was small comfort, but he understood something now. The radical changes in Kathleen had their roots in the loss of her baby, he was sure.

He knew, too, that their weekend idyll had been shattered. He stayed until after nine, but they were unable to recapture their closeness. Kathleen remained drawn and subdued, attempting to carry on a conversation over dinner while her mind was obviously elsewhere. Quinn watched her retreat farther and farther from him, and tried desperately to bring her back. He talked of Patrick and their school days, recounting every amusing incident he could recall. For his efforts he got a few wan smiles that didn't alter the bleakness in her eyes. Nothing seemed to touch her.

Finally, in desperation, he tried to make love to her. She was unresponsive. Frustrated, he blurted out, "Were you married?"

They were on the couch, Kathleen lying with her head resting on the arm. She looked at him blankly. He sat up, wanting to shake her until her eyes lost that closed expression.

"To Lauren's father," he persisted.

She sat up, too, pulling her kimono together, as though the silk fabric offered some protection. "No."

He knew that he shouldn't have brought it up again, but damn it, he was grasping at straws, trying to crack her defenses. "I'm sorry. I know you don't want to talk about it."

She clasped her hands together in her lap and studied them. "I really can't, Quinn. I need to be alone now, if you wouldn't mind."

He didn't argue. He was defeated. "I'll be out of town this week on business." The news seemed to make no impression on her. "I'll call you."

"All right. Good night, Quinn."

He left to try to patch up his wounded ego. Why wouldn't she talk to him? As he drove away, an answer came to him. She didn't trust him. She'd been betrayed by a man she'd loved, Lauren's father, and she wasn't going to trust another man easily.

For a while this weekend she'd let down the barriers and allowed him in—until he'd found Lauren's picture, and the barriers had snapped back in place, doors closed, locks secured. You didn't change an attitude built up over the years in a single weekend, no matter how splendid the lovemaking.

Chapter Ten

She knew it now, if she hadn't before. Quinn was the love of her life. There would never be anyone else for her.

How else could she explain the weekend? In the week that followed, she relived their lovemaking often, the memories making her feel weak. It was more than the sex, so much more. Because of her love for Quinn, she had revealed too much of herself. She wasn't a woman who confided easily, yet she'd told him about Lauren, something she'd never told another living soul. True, she hadn't told him everything, but she'd revealed too much nevertheless. Having gone so far, she knew she would have to finish the job eventually. Quinn wasn't going to stop until he knew everything.

She spent the week trying to decide how best to tell him, how to make it as easy as possible for both of them.

While he was in Spain, where he'd gone on a buying trip, he phoned her twice. The long-distance conversations were stilted, full of pregnant pauses between the dialogue, unsatisfactory for both of them. During the second call he said, "I'll be back in town next Tuesday. Can I see you Tuesday evening?"

"Yes. I'll have a stack of forms for you to fill out. Come to dinner at seven." She had been working with Immigration all week, working her way through the maze of red tape that was required to bring Van into the country. In spite of her resolve not to become emotionally involved, she was developing feelings for the boy. She told herself it was only natural, since she was spending so much time working on his case. Once the job was done and the child was safely with his father, she could forget him. Could she also forget Quinn? She didn't know the answer to that. For a woman who liked to be in control of her life it was frustrating—and frightening.

She made plans to go out to dinner with Maggie Friday night. They dressed casually and went to a small restaurant in the neighborhood.

"I'm glad you were free this evening," Kathleen remarked over dinner. "I thought Bert might be coming to town again."

"He has business to take care of this weekend," Maggie said. "Actually, I didn't want him to come again so soon. We need some time apart to think about our relationship."

"Does thinking help?" Kathleen asked dryly.

Maggie smiled. "Not much."

"What's the problem? I thought you and Bert were getting along famously."

"Oh, we are. That's the problem. I mean, how can you be sure you love somebody when things happen so fast?"

"I suppose, if it's really love, it doesn't take long."

"What really scares me is that I'm afraid Bert is thinking about marriage."

"That would seem to be the logical next step," Kathleen said with a grin. "No insult intended, Maggie, but you're not the mistress type."

Maggie eyed her thoughtfully. "Neither are you, my friend."

Obviously the time Quinn had been spending at her house had not gone unnoticed. Kathleen gave a shaky little laugh. "I know. I'm going to have to do something about getting my life back on track again soon."

"Back in the old rut, you mean? Listen, Kathleen, I used to think you just weren't very interested in men, the way you brushed them off right and left. Since you've been seeing Quinn, I've changed my mind. Now I think he's the only man for you. If you can't have him, you don't want anybody. I guess what I'm trying to say is, don't do anything rash. If you love the guy, you can surely work it out."

"Isn't this a bit like the pot calling the kettle black?"

Maggie shook her head. "When I'm sure I'm in love with Bert and not merely flattered by his attention, I'll know what to do. Now stop diverting the conversation from yourself. You're not going to tell me you don't love Quinn, are you?"

"Oh, Maggie, it's not that simple," Kathleen sighed.

"Love rarely is. But denying it isn't the answer."

"Sometimes it may be." Kathleen hadn't realized until that moment how much she had been holding inside and how desperately she needed to talk about it. Almost before she knew it, she was pouring out the story of Quinn and Mai and Van. "Okay, so maybe I am in love with Quinn," she concluded finally. "The trouble is that we're not the only two people involved. Van will probably be here in a few weeks, and he's going to need all Quinn's love and attention." She thrust her fork into her spaghetti, as though to emphasize her words. "I cannot come between that child and his father." She took a bracing breath. "I've gotten too involved with the boy already, and I haven't even met him."

Maggie stared at her, shaking her head. "No wonder you're getting involved. You've got so much love to give, it has to come out somehow. Why do you fight it? I don't understand you, Kathleen."

Of course Maggie didn't understand. She didn't know about the baby Kathleen had loved and battled to keep, then lost. Love for a child was such a pervasive thing; its tentacles wrapped themselves around the deepest parts of you—heart and soul and marrow—and settled in for a lifetime's stay. It could destroy you when those tentacles were ruthlessly severed. Maggie had never experienced that destruction, so she couldn't understand Kathleen's self-protective need to refuse to give her patched-up heart to another person's child. The potential pain was too great to risk.

"You'll simply have to take my word for it, Maggie. It wouldn't work."

A fierce early summer thunderstorm pelted the city, then settled down to a steady rain. The storm had delayed Quinn's flight for almost two hours. He stopped at his house only long enough to leave his luggage before going to Kathleen. It had been a horrendous ten days since he'd seen her. Much of the weekend they'd spent together had grown vague in his mind, like a dream that quickly blurs upon awakening. The park, her bedroom, the meadow where they'd picnicked—they were all fuzzy in his memory. But her body beneath his, the dark passion in her eyes, her soft, knowing smile—those things were vivid enough to arouse him anew every time he thought of them.

He'd made love to her fiercely, without a bit of finesse, like a wild man, and finally, when he'd regained a little control, slowly and gently until her body trembled with an overload of sensations. He had seen her as frenzied as he was with sheer animal need, all fire and power, and again so soft and giving that it made his throat ache with tenderness.

Increasingly, over the years, he'd grown sure he had exaggerated his memories of her to the point where no flesh-and-blood woman could live up to them. He'd known his share of women intimately, and none of them had ever elicited the wonder that had characterized that night beside the lake when Kathleen was seventeen. During his imprisonment his memories of her had been his salvation. Kathleen was his ideal woman, so he put her safely on a pedestal and left her there. A man needs his fantasies, he'd told himself, but he'd be stupid to mix them up with reality.

When he'd learned Mai was dead, he'd known he had to see Kathleen again. Having seen her, he'd known he had to make love to her. She wasn't the girl he remembered, but the differences in her had challenged him. The more she pulled back from him, the more she haunted him. When the physical capitulation finally came, she had stunned him. She was both less and more than his fantasies. Less idol, and more woman.

Quinn frowned as he negotiated the freeway, driving through the downpour as fast as he dared. The knowledge that she'd loved another man enough to bear his child had really knocked the props from under him. He knew it was unreasonable to expect her not to have formed any deep attachment while they were apart, but his feelings didn't respond to reason. While he had been thinking that he'd broken through all her defenses, there had been more layers that he hadn't even suspected. Her refusal to talk about it had occupied much of his thoughts for the past ten days. It was as though she wanted to protect Lauren's father somehow. Did that mean she still loved him? He was aware that if he pressured her on the subject he might not like the answers he got, but he had to know. At least then he'd know what he had to contend with. Anything was better than the doubt and apprehension he'd been suffering. Wasn't it?

Kathleen was as nervous as a cat by seven o'clock. She'd made the mistake of getting herself ready and completing the dinner preparations an hour too soon. Then she'd had nothing to do but think.

The weekend with Quinn provided ample material for meditation, some of it erotic, some warm, and some so disturbing that she wondered how she was going to get through the evening. As a girl she had given him everything; in all the time since, she had never stopped loving him.

But he had gone halfway around the world and fallen in love with Mai.

Grow up, Kathleen, she ordered herself. What do you expect of a man, any man? Wishing that things had turned out differently would bring her nothing but pain. Life wasn't a romantic novel with all the misunderstandings cleared up and things settled to everyone's satisfaction on the last page. Hadn't she spent the past fifteen years ridding herself of romantic dreams and naïveté?

Perhaps he *did* love her in his way, but she would always be second best. There was a small, twisting pain in her stomach at the acknowledgment, but she had learned how to deal with pain. No, she reminded herself, she couldn't let it happen to her again. She couldn't afford to.

It was all very well to tell herself these things while she was alone, but when she opened the door to Quinn, he stunned her by hauling her into his arms before she could close the door. His hair was damp from the rain. "I missed you," he said roughly. "You'll never know how much I missed you. Did you miss me?"

"I—"

"If you didn't, I don't want to know." While she stared, wide-eyed, he lowered his head and kissed her with a devastating hunger. She didn't move or speak when he lifted his head again. Quinn took a steadying breath and asked, "How many men did you go out with while I was gone?"

"None."

He grinned with delight. "What smells so good?"

Without waiting for her reply he released her and headed for the kitchen, leaving her to stare after him. Dazed, Kathleen touched her fingers to her lips, wondering if she had dreamed that hot, demanding kiss.

Confused, she followed him to the kitchen, thinking that she had to get things in hand right away.

He was peering through the glass oven door. "Ham?"

"Ham loaf. With new potatoes." She took an apron from a drawer and tied it around her waist, over her yellow silk dress. "While I'm getting everything on the table, you can start on those forms. They're on the bar."

He sat on a stool, reading and filling in the forms, while Kathleen went back and forth between table and kitchen. Whenever she passed the bar she studied him surreptitiously. He was bent over, concentrating and writing hurriedly, as though he wanted to finish quickly. She hadn't realized how much she'd missed him until he'd walked into her house; she could admit that in her private thoughts. What would she do if he kissed her like that again? *When,* she corrected herself. When he kissed her like that again.

No point in trying to convince herself she could stop loving him. Loving Quinn was a given. So, what next? Well, she knew the pitfalls that came with loving him. This time she had her eyes wide open. This time she knew where to draw the line. If she found herself stepping over the line, she'd think about Mai. That would be her defense of last resort.

"Dinner's ready," she said a few minutes later.

"I'm just finishing these." He signed his name once more, capped the pen and laid it on the bar, and walked into the dining room to pull out her chair for her.

She shot him a look and sat down. She was too aware of his closeness behind her, and her heart fluttered. As she reached for her napkin, he bent his head and brushed his lips over her temple. She couldn't resist turning to look at him. As she gazed into those deep-blue eyes, she felt her head begin to swim. If he had seduction in mind, she was afraid he wasn't going to find her much of a challenge.

He took her breath away, just the sight and scent of him. He lifted a finger and ran it over the curve of her cheek. She couldn't think straight when he touched her. And when he looked at her like that, his eyes knowing, his lips tilted in a sensuous half smile, her mind filled with thoughts of his naked flesh against hers, of the place beyond the stars where no other man had ever taken her.

"Quinn." She put a hand up to brush the cheek he had just touched. She didn't know if she meant to stop the tingling left by his finger or hold it close to savor it. If he touched her again… But he dropped his hand and went around the table to sit down.

"This looks delicious."

"Thank you." She studied him with veiled curiosity. What was he thinking?

When he glanced up and met her look she was rather relieved by the uncertainty she saw in his eyes. He wasn't as sure of himself as she'd imagined.

"How are the lovebirds next door getting along?" Quinn asked. It seemed a safe enough topic, one that would erase the wariness in her eyes.

"They're taking a vacation from each other right now," she said in a quiet tone, "to think about their relationship."

He remembered the way the man had looked at the woman that Saturday morning when he'd asked them where he could find Kathleen. He remembered that he'd thought they'd been married for years and how great it was that the man still looked at his wife in that adoring way. "She having doubts?"

"She doesn't want to be rushed."

"Love is not a patient emotion."

"I'm afraid I can't speak with much authority about that."

"Didn't you love him?"

She knew he meant Lauren's father. Her eyes were eloquent, but her voice was steady. "Yes, but it wasn't enough."

"Enough to bear his child."

"That's true. But because he was gone, I turned all my emotions on Lauren. I wanted her to be my life. That's a selfish kind of love."

His eyes, steady on her face, were gentle. The man had deserted her, then. "Do you blame yourself because she died?"

"Sometimes." She didn't want to talk about Lauren now. Maybe later she'd have more courage. "Do you blame yourself for Mai's death?" she countered.

"No." He shook his head. "She decided not to go to the embassy, to stay in her house with Van. I couldn't force her to go. I wasn't even there for weeks before she died."

A part of her cringed away from hearing him speak of his wife, but ignoring something didn't make it go away. She thought that if she knew more about Mai, it would help her understand why Quinn had loved the other woman. He seemed more willing to talk about her than when she'd questioned him before. "What was she like?"

He started to answer curtly, to change the subject. But if he wanted her to talk to him about Lauren's father, he'd have to be as candid as he could about Mai. He shook off his reluctance. "She was a good person. Very loyal. Very courageous."

"How did you meet her?"

"She was a teacher in a school for young children. On Saturday nights she used to go with a group of friends to a bar where American servicemen hung out in Saigon." He hoped she wouldn't notice that he hadn't answered directly. "She'd left her family in the country to work in Saigon. She was really pretty naive. She wasn't a whore."

"I didn't think she was. I know she was special or you wouldn't have fallen in love with her."

All of a sudden he couldn't meet her gaze. He buttered a roll and applied himself to eating with a concentration that seemed deliberate. She wondered, as she studied him, what that first meeting between him and Mai had been like. She pictured a dim, dingy, noisy bar filled with boisterous American soldiers and exotic Vietnamese girls. Many of the women would have been prostitutes, she knew. But Mai had obviously been different. She'd been educated, a teacher. Kathleen wondered if Quinn had looked into her eyes and known immediately that Mai would be important to him.

"What are you thinking about?"

He looked up abruptly, almost overturning his glass, as though he'd forgotten where he was. "I was thinking," he began, sipping from his wineglass, "how best to explain Mai to you." Without telling you the most important thing about her, he added grimly to himself. He was still wary of revealing the whole story even to Kathleen, until Van was on American soil. "She needed somebody to take care of her. When her parents found out she'd taken up with an American serviceman, they disowned her. And then, when her pregnancy became known among her co-workers, she lost her job."

He spoke slowly, as though he were choosing his words with care. He hadn't spoken of love, she noted. Perhaps he was being kind, not wanting to hurt her.

"You were all she had."

"Yes, and the government allotment was her only income." He tasted his wine again. It was a red, warm and rich. Seductive. He was reminded of the taste of Kathleen's mouth during that one brief kiss of the evening. "From what you said a minute ago, you know it can be a burden to be somebody's entire world."

It was an odd thing for him to say. Had Mai become too clinging, too demanding, after she'd lost her family and job? A desperate woman might react that way. She must have been terrified that he would abandon her, too. "You do feel guilty, after all."

"I suppose I could, if I let myself dwell on it." He studied her over the rim of his glass. The light from the chandelier revealed golden highlights in her shining sable hair. She'd pinned her hair back away from her face, exposing the delicately feminine shape of her ears and the small gold studs at the lobes. Highlighted by dark mascara, her lashes looked incredibly long and thick, and she wore a soft rose gloss on her lips. The clinging yellow silk dress was perfect on her. She knew how to play up her attractions. A man could lose himself in looking at her. "But I don't let myself," he continued after a moment. "Saigon and Mai were part of another life that I'd like to forget ever existed."

"But you can't forget it entirely, because Van exists."

"Yes," Quinn said so quietly that a chill ran through her.

Van would be with him soon, and every time Quinn looked at him, he'd see Mai. The past had a way of intruding into the present, no matter how determined you were to hold it back. She asked no further questions about Mai. She knew all she needed to know. Quinn felt her withdrawal and pondered how to overcome it. They finished the meal, and the patter of rain on the roof seemed to grow louder in the silence. Kathleen got up to clear the table.

"Would you like coffee?"

He shook his head, watching her. Slowly he rose and came around the table. He took the plate she was holding and set it back on the table.

"I want to make love to you."

It was hardly a revelation. What he wanted had been in his eyes during dinner, but the naked declaration left her shaken. "We need to talk."

His hand tightened on her arm when she tried to turn away. "We've been talking, and I've felt you slipping away from me."

She was incapable of pulling back. Her own need was too strong. She looked up at him, and fighting her feelings suddenly became more than she was capable of. "I know."

He saw the pulse pounding at the base of her throat. This evidence of her response to his touch thrilled him. Slowly he pulled the pins from her hair. "When you look at me like that, I know you want me, too." Her hair fell forward, dark and heavy.

She felt weak, her limbs numb. "I didn't say I don't want you." Her voice was low, husky. "But we have to talk first." It seemed imperative that she tell him the truth about Lauren now. In some ways it would be a relief to tell him. Perhaps she wanted to shift some of her guilt to his shoulders; she didn't know.

He buried his hands in her hair, and her eyes darkened. "Nothing we could say can compare with this." His mouth took hers in fierce possession. Kathleen wound her arms around his neck and lifted her body to his. He was right. This was what she wanted.

They'd make love until they were spent. After he heard what she had to tell him, he might be so angry that he'd leave and never come back. This might be the last time they would be together like this, and she needed it.

Breathless, she broke the kiss and led him to the bedroom. In silence they undressed with the clumsy haste of overpowering physical desire. The rain hammered against the windows, and a deep, moonless darkness cloaked the room. When he touched her a fever of impatience prickled over her skin. She ran her hands over the hard breadth of his shoulders and down to the small of his back. An equal impatience shuddered through him. He slid his hand up her naked back until his fingers curved around the nape of her neck. "You're all I thought about while I was gone, all I dreamed about."

His body moved against hers, his need hard and throbbing. She wrapped her arms around his waist and pressed closer. "Love me now," she pleaded.

All thought of the skillful prolonging of pleasure fled as his mouth came down on hers. The storm that roared in them outdid the one that flashed and raged outside. Wracked by the erupting power of the inner storm, they fell onto the bed together.

Hot flesh to hot flesh, they clung to each other, their mouths devouring, their hands greedy. We're mad, Kathleen thought during the brief instant when she could think at all; this is a sickness. She arched against him, and he answered her need by lifting her hips in his hands and burying himself in her body. For a moment he held still, breathing raggedly, fighting to regain a remnant of control and bank the raging passion.

She wanted nothing of control, neither his nor hers. She reveled in the cords of muscle in his back, his lean flanks, the heat of his blood pulsing just below his skin. She lifted herself against him once more, and he gasped and forgot everything but the whirlpool that was irresistibly drawing him in. Together they were hurled into the mighty tide, lost and spinning. Then they were gripped by twin explosions of sensation, and their bodies were thrown, battered and shuddering, down the final descent.

Was it seconds or hours later when he lifted his weight from her and drew her tenderly against him? "I'll make you forget him," he vowed huskily.

She snuggled sleepily against him. "Who?"

"Lauren's father." His hand smoothed her tousled hair. "I don't want any other man in your head. Never again."

She was silent for a long moment, trying to swallow the clump of tears in her throat. "There's never been any man in my head but you."

His hand on her hair stilled. She could sense him trying to understand her meaning.

She drew a shaky breath, knowing that the moment had come. "You're Lauren's father, Quinn."

Chapter Eleven

Perhaps it was the sheer release of finally saying the words, or the deafening lash of rain against the windows and the sudden fury of thunder and lightning, or Quinn's explosive reaction. She was assaulted by a vague montage of memories that left her shaking, as though she were under life-threatening siege. There were images of Lauren, of her parents, and sensations of fear, guilt and despair, all coming at her at once.

Quinn, naked and pacing, was illuminated like some angry god by blinding flashes of lightning. He was in a state of shock, she told herself, as she sat up in bed and pulled the sheet around her.

Why? He kept asking the question silently and shaking his head at the incomprehensibility of it. Why had she kept this from him for so long? She had no right! Even though Lauren had been dead for two years before Kathleen knew he was alive? Even then!

When she tried to tell him that she had only wanted to forget what had happened, he retorted that her feelings hadn't been the only ones to be considered. He had been equally involved.

He roamed to a window, then whirled toward her. "It wasn't right, Kathleen." He went on in the same vein until she felt helpless and incapable of making him understand. Then the thunder crashed, shaking the house, and another bolt of lightning lit the room with a terrifying, white flash. Hugging herself, Kathleen began to sob.

In the pitch dark Quinn stumbled into a chair and finally found his way back to the bed by following the sounds of her weeping. "Kath. Don't do that, please." But she only wept more wildly. "Come here, love."

When he touched her, she threw herself into his arms and clung. From the way she was shivering the room might have been icy instead of too warm and humid. Her skin felt cold. Quinn pulled the coverlet over her and cuddled her. "Shh, sweetheart, I'm sorry. I didn't mean to be so hard on you." He patted and stroked her until the trembling eased and her sobs died down to silent tears.

"Don't move." She pressed her wet face into his bare shoulder. "Please don't let go of me." She gulped air into her starving lungs; it burned her swollen throat as it went down. "Oh, Quinn, I didn't know what to do. I was seventeen and pregnant and virtually alone. I didn't know where to turn for help."

He rocked her gently, holding her head so that her cheek pressed against his shoulder. "Why didn't you go to Patrick?"

"They made me promise not to," she murmured as a shudder ran through her. He held her tighter in response, stroking the curve of her back. "They said I'd let them down, shamed them.... They only seemed concerned with how my pregnancy was going to affect them. They were disappointed. They were ashamed. They said if I didn't want them to disown me, I had to do exactly as they said. I'd never seen that vengeful side of them before. I'd always needed their approval so much that I didn't give them any reason to punish me. Maybe I realized, without being consciously aware of it, that their love had strings attached. I had to continually be earning it. When I told them I was pregnant they... they changed. They were like two strangers." She turned her face into his shoulder again and squeezed her eyes shut on fresh tears. Her fingers dug into the hard muscles of his back. "At first they tried to make me tell them who the father was. I wouldn't. They thought I'd break down if they kept at me long enough, but when they finally saw I wasn't ever going to tell them... I think they actually hated me."

Kathleen paused to wipe her cheeks with a corner of the sheet. Outside the storm continued to rage, but in Quinn's arms she felt warm and comforted.

"I knew if I told them the truth they'd never forgive you. They would have convinced themselves that you'd forced me.... I could never have made them believe I was half to blame. They wanted me to keep on being their perfect little girl. They couldn't stand the thought of seeing me growing big with the baby, so they banished me from their sight. I went to stay with Mother's sister in Florida." She paused, remembering how lost she'd felt, stepping off the plane, not even sure she'd recognize her aunt. "They told Patrick it was my idea to go, that I wanted Mom to spend all her time caring for Dad. Aunt Ada had never married. I don't think she liked men much. The poor woman was hardly the person to deal with an unmarried, pregnant teenager. But my parents had helped her financially, and I'm sure she felt obligated to take me."

Her tears had slowed, and her arms were no longer clinging. She was simply exhausted; her emotional outburst had drained her. She didn't move when another crack of thunder rattled the windows.

"Kath." Quinn lowered her to the bed, then lay down beside her. He took her face in his hands and tried to make out her features in the dark. "You should have told them that I was the baby's father. You shouldn't have had to bear the brunt of their anger alone."

In a brief flicker of lightning he saw her eyes, shining and swollen, staring at him. She shook her head and sighed wearily. He realized that she was already regretting exposing so much of her pain to him; the words had tumbled out of her while she was too vulnerable to realize what she was saying. But they couldn't be called back now.

"I couldn't see what good it would do." Restlessly, she sat up again. She dragged her hands through her hair and hugged her knees to her chest. "By the time I knew I was pregnant, you'd already been reported missing in action."

Pondering her words, he sat on the side of the bed and turned on the lamp. He searched for his briefs and undershirt and put them on. Then he leaned back against the headboard. "Was it better in Florida?"

She shrugged. "I suppose. Aunt Ada didn't exactly approve of me, but she didn't try to lay another guilt trip on me. She just went around clucking over me. Did I feel okay? Had I remembered to take my vitamins?"

"You got along with her?" he asked. She was staring at the stormy night beyond the window.

Kathleen rested her chin on her knees, remembering her prim Aunt Ada, who hadn't known quite what to do with the niece who'd been dumped on her doorstep. She felt so tired, but she knew she couldn't stop now until he knew it all. "She tried to be kind, but having me there totally disrupted her life. I enrolled in school, and she bought me a wedding ring at the dime store and told me to say I'd been married briefly, but my husband had been killed in some kind of accident. I did as she asked. I thought if it would make her feel any better, why not?" A faint smile touched Kathleen's mouth. "After I'd been in school a week, the school counselor called Aunt Ada to suggest that I get therapy. It wasn't normal, the counselor said, for a teenager to be so quiet and withdrawn. Aunt Ada said that if she was widowed and pregnant at seventeen, she'd be withdrawn, too. All I needed was time to deal with my grief, Ada said, and she'd thank the counselor to mind her own business. So there was no more talk of my getting counseling."

She paused and closed her eyes to alleviate the burning caused by the flood of tears. "My parents wouldn't have approved of my talking to an outsider about my personal problems. I'd made my bed, and I was expected to lie in it. Over and over Aunt Ada told me I'd have to give the baby away. I knew she was acting under instructions, because my mother wrote almost every week, saying the same thing. The letters were full of how my father had ruined his health working hard to give me and Patrick advantages, and how what I'd done had broken his heart, not to mention nearly killing him. The only thing I'd left them, my mother said, was their good name in the community, and if I came back with a baby that would be destroyed, too. So I had to give the baby up for adoption before I came home."

Her words trailed off, and she didn't respond when Quinn placed a comforting hand on her shoulder. He watched the shine of the lamplight on her tousled hair.

"I tried to see their viewpoint; I really did. I told myself the baby would be better off with two parents who loved it. I still had to finish high school after the baby was born, and even with a diploma it would be difficult for me to earn enough to support myself and a child. But the closer the time for the birth came, the surer I was that I couldn't give the baby away. Maybe I wanted to show my folks they'd pushed me as far as they could. I know now it was selfish of me—"

"Kath."

"Let me finish this while I can." She took a breath, braced herself and continued. "After Lauren was born I called Mother and told her my decision. I begged her to let me come home until I finished high school. I promised I'd find a way to take care of Lauren on my own after I graduated. She wouldn't agree at first. There were several phone conversations with my aunt. I guess Ada convinced Mother that I wasn't going to change my mind. Or maybe that I couldn't stay with her any longer. When Lauren was a month old Mother said we could come home for four months, until I graduated. I'll never forget how I felt when I carried Lauren into the house. The atmosphere was thick with disapproval. Dad just stared at me with a look in his eyes that said, How could you do this to us? I laid Lauren down in my old crib—Mother had brought it down from the attic. Mother walked in, took one look at Lauren and walked out again without saying a word. But she agreed to baby-sit while I was in school. I saw that as a big concession. I told myself she wouldn't be able to take care of Lauren without falling in love with her. And maybe she would have . . . if Dad hadn't had another coronary.''

Her throat closed, and she bowed her head and pressed her hands over her face until she regained her composure. "He died without regaining consciousness,'' she went on resolutely, and it seemed to get easier with each word. She spoke more quickly now, wanting to get it over with. "He didn't suffer, the doctor said. But Mother was simply devastated, and she turned on me. I was responsible for Dad's death, she said. I'd killed him.''

"Oh, God. . . .'' Quinn tried to pull her back into his arms, but she resisted, and his hands fell away.

"She just couldn't deal with her grief, and she went a little crazy, I think. She was like a zombie. Some days she never even changed out of her nightgown. I'd run home at lunch to feed Lauren because I was afraid Mother would forget. I should have dropped out of school. But there were only eight weeks left until graduation. I knew Mother wouldn't deliberately hurt Lauren. She might let her cry or wear a wet diaper, but I told myself that wouldn't do any permanent damage. Every day, when I got home from school, I'd hold her and talk to her for hours, trying to make up for Mother's lack of attention. I'd tell her how happy we'd be once I got a job and we had our own home, the places we'd go and the things we'd do. She would coo and smile at me, and she was getting fat. She seemed fine." Kathleen let out a shaky sigh. "I came home from school one afternoon and Mother was in the living room in her nightgown, just rocking and staring out the window. I asked her how Lauren was, and she said she'd been asleep ever since I put her to bed after lunch, that she hadn't heard a peep out of her. I went into the baby's room. She was lying on her stomach, and she'd kicked her blanket off. I must have stood there for a full minute, looking at her, before I realized that something was wrong. I—I touched her, and her skin felt cold." She bowed her head so that her forehead touched her knees. She shivered and hugged her legs tighter. "So cold," she murmured.

Quinn wrapped his arms around her. Ignoring her huddled withdrawal, he pulled her against his side and rested his chin on her head. The storm was dying. Rain still fell, but not with the same pelting fury as before.

"I turned her over—she wasn't breathing. I screamed for mother to call an ambulance. I picked her up and gave her mouth-to-mouth until the medics came. At the hospital they told me she'd died of crib death, and that she'd probably been dead for more than an hour before I tried to revive her. Mother hadn't gone in to check on her. She hadn't even thought about her. She sat there, rocking, while Lauren died."

Quinn's arms tightened around her. "Honey, don't . . ."

Her tears began to flow again, and Kathleen didn't try to stop them. "I hated Mother. But I loved her, too. She was so pitiful, refusing to make any kind of life without Dad. I wanted to blame her for Lauren's death, but I knew I was more at fault than she was." Her shoulders heaved, and for a few moments she couldn't go on. When she did, her voice was filled with bitterness and self-recrimination. "I knew Mother wasn't behaving normally, and she'd never wanted to take care of Lauren in the first place. She didn't love her. Lauren was just a nuisance that she had agreed to put up with for a while. I should never have left Lauren with Mother after Dad died." Her words were separated by short sobs. She pressed the heels of her hands against her closed eyelids. "I wished I had died instead of Lauren." Her words trembled out, barely understandable. "She was so beautiful, so perfect. It wasn't fair. She deserved two mature parents who would have cared for her properly. Because I couldn't bear to give her up, I denied her that. If I hadn't insisted on keeping her, or if I'd stayed at home and taken care of her myself, she might not have died."

She was only partially aware that he was lifting her from the bed, the coverlet still wrapped around her. He carried her to a chair and sat down, cradling her against him. "Kathleen, you know that's nonsense. You couldn't watch her every minute. Unless you'd been standing over her when she stopped breathing and had known exactly what to do, she would still have died. You can't blame yourself."

She shook her head, then dropped it to his shoulder. "Yes, I can. I should have been there." Taking a deep breath, she settled more closely against him. "I'm responsible for the death of my baby. Our baby."

"Kath." There was pain as well as helplessness in his voice.

"I know all the arguments for why I shouldn't feel responsible. Sometimes I can convince myself that they're valid. I was too young to raise a baby by myself, and too ignorant to know it, but my intentions were the best. I was going to be a superwoman. I was going to get a job and make enough to hire the best baby-sitter I could find and, when Lauren was older, I was going to put her in the best day-care center. I was going to find a little house and decorate her room in pink and white. I was going to read to her every day and give her piano and ballet lessons when she was old enough." She gripped his shoulders as the cruel irony of her words flooded through her. "I was going to work wonders and show Mother and Aunt Ada how much they'd underestimated me."

Quinn brushed back her hair and dried her cheek with his fingers. "You loved Lauren; that's all that really counts." His voice was low and sure, and he could feel her relax against him.

"I loved her well, but not wisely. And don't tell me that no seventeen-year-old girl has lived long enough to be wise. I know that with my mind, yet my emotions won't let me off that easily. But I think about it less and less as time goes by."

"I've made you remember it all again."

She sighed and continued, "I needed to tell you. You were a part of it, too." She listened to the steady, now comforting, drum of rain on the windows. "Somehow I managed to collect my thoughts well enough to get through finals and graduate. Dad's will left half the insurance money to Mother, and a quarter each to Patrick and me. The day after my high school graduation I enrolled in summer school at the University of Texas. Maybe I should have stayed home and tried to help Mother, but she didn't want my help. I practically dragged her to a counselor once, but she refused to go again. And I knew that if I didn't get away from her, I'd go crazy. So I gave a neighbor my phone number in Austin, asked her to look in on Mother now and then, and left. I loved my classes and made new friends. It was like being let out of jail."

Kathleen freed herself from Quinn's hold, found a nightgown and dropped it over her head. She began to pace, the silk fabric of the gown clinging and shifting with her movements. "As long as I could keep my mind full of studies and college activities, I didn't brood. In August, just before the start of my sophomore year at U.T., we got word of Patrick's death. I was with Mother all the time those first few days. She didn't cry or even talk about him. I'm not even sure she understood what had happened." She stopped at a window, bracing her hands on the sill. "I put her in a nursing home, where she would at least have three meals a day and medical attention. But she didn't get any better. Every time I saw her she was thinner and more withdrawn. I put her under the care of a different doctor every time I went home, hoping that one of them could help her. I pleaded with her to cooperate with the doctors; I talked until I ran out of words, but nothing changed. She just faded away before my eyes. She died during my senior year at U.T., and all I felt was numb. She'd been dying for years; she wanted to die." She turned to face him and gave him a long look as though trying to fathom what he was making of her words. "I sold the house and stayed at U.T. to get a master's degree in business. I worked in Austin until I took the job with Congressman Smythe."

He came to her, turning her so the lamplight fell on her face. "You did what you had to do." She didn't respond, and he frowned, studying her. "I hate it that you had to go through it alone. It wasn't your fault, none of it."

"I know that. Really, I do, only..." She broke off and would have turned away, but his hands held her.

"No onlys. I can't change the past, Kath. If I could, we'd go back and I'd be with you, helping you. But we have the future. Let me spend it with you." His hands framed her face, and his eyes held hers. "I love you, Kath."

He kissed her then, and for a moment she let it happen. It was so easy to stop fighting, to turn her back on the past, to let everything go. But her past was as much a part of her as the present. Its lessons had been learned the hard way. She broke free. For an instant she gazed into his eyes, feeling the deep ache of desire. Then she turned her back on him, on her feelings.

"Say yes, Kath," he whispered. "We can start over. We can have a life together."

She stood unmoving for a short time before she shook her bowed head. "I can't make any promises, Quinn. Don't ask me too."

His hands gripped her, forcing her around to face him. "Why? I know you still have feelings for me."

"It's not a question of my feelings for you."

His hands tightened on her arms. "For God's sake, what is it then?"

"If I've learned anything during the past fifteen years, it's that—when everything's said and done— there's nobody to depend on but myself."

"That," he said in a tight voice, "is rubbish."

"Let me go." The request was toneless.

He released her, frustrated and angry. Would he ever understand her? He watched her walk to the bureau, stare at a small painting on the wall and half turn so that her face was visible in profile. "If it weren't for Van, maybe we could start over."

His hands hung helplessly at his sides. He balled them into fists. "I don't see what one thing has to do with the other."

"Van exists," she went on, as if he hadn't spoken. "He's going to need every scrap of love and attention you've got. Children always pay the worst price for the mistakes of the adults around them. This move will be traumatic for him. He doesn't need me in the picture, complicating his life even more."

"The three of us can start over together. There'll never be a better time for us."

Perhaps she was imagining it, but the way he put it sounded so clinical, so planned. If he really loved her, why hadn't he gotten in touch with her long before he needed her help with Van? He wanted a mother for Van now; in that sense it *would* be the perfect time for them to start over. But she wasn't Van's mother. She would be only a substitute for the woman Quinn had married. And what if Van wouldn't accept her? What if he resented her presence in Quinn's life? It would be a completely understandable reaction. She could be setting herself up to be hurt again. She shook her head. "No."

"You're a coward. You've had a bad time, so you're afraid to get involved with life again." His voice was cold, accusing.

Her head snapped around. "You have no right to judge me! I lost a baby, Patrick, my parents—you don't know what it was like. You don't know anything about it."

"I lost a baby, too."

"A fact that you've known for all of twenty minutes!"

The hint of contempt in her words infuriated him. "And whose fault is that?"

She stared at him. She was already carrying around all the guilt she could handle. She wasn't about to take any more from him. "Go home, Quinn. Neither of us is in any condition to discuss this right now."

"That's your answer to everything, isn't it? Turn your back. Run away from it." Rigid with anger, he dressed, his movements jerky and quick. Without another word he walked out of the bedroom and the house.

She didn't move until she heard the roar of his engine over the sound of the rain. She went to the window. The yard light provided weak illumination, but enough for her to watch his car back out, jerk to a halt, then shoot forward and speed down the street. He couldn't have picked a more hurtful parting shot. The echo of his words still hung in the room. She clenched a fist and pressed it against her mouth.

Quinn was partly right. Going so far from home to college had been running away. But there had been no way for her to deal with what was happening at home, and leaving had been the only way for her to survive. Kathleen relaxed her fingers and ran them through her hair. Her eyes burned, and she felt the beginnings of a headache. She stared out at the night.

She had left home, and she had survived. Slowly she had made another life for herself in Austin, and then she'd moved to Oklahoma City, where she had shaped a nice, neat existence for herself. Quinn had come back into her life only long enough to make her thoroughly miserable.

He hadn't really needed her to bring Van to American. He could have dealt with Immigration directly. He wanted her to be a mother to his son. The temper that had flared at Quinn was gone now, leaving only the weight of sadness.

She resented Quinn for disrupting her world again. She resented the fact that he seemed to have taken it for granted that she still wanted him. But... She sighed softly and turned away from the window. He'd said he loved her, but how could she give him her heart again?

The question remained unanswered in the days that followed, during which she didn't hear from Quinn. She worked long hours and tried not to think about him. She wanted to be so tired when she fell into bed at night that she wouldn't lie awake, remembering the past few weeks. When he finally did call, early in June, his voice was cool, the voice of a stranger. Clearly he was still angry with her. Perhaps he had expected her to make the first move to heal the breach.

"What's the status of Van's immigration?" he inquired without any preliminary amenities.

Kathleen gripped the receiver and bit her lip at the unexpected jolt the sound of his voice caused. "Things are moving along. You wouldn't believe the red tape. You'll have to be patient."

"How hard are you trying to cut through the red tape, Kathleen?"

The implied insult hurt her. Her knees trembled, and she lowered herself into the chair at her desk. "What are you suggesting?"

"It occurred to me that you might not be trying as hard as you could. Wouldn't you really prefer it if Van didn't come here at all?"

Her temper erupted. "That's a lie! How can you—"

He cut into her argument. "If I don't hear something positive from you within a week, I'll go around you and contact Immigration myself."

"Maybe you should have done that in the first place!" She slammed down the receiver and gripped the edge of the desk with both hands. She was shaking all over.

Chapter Twelve

Renee buzzed through to Kathleen's office. "Mr. Drewly's on the line." More than a week had passed since Quinn had phoned and issued his ultimatum. Kathleen wondered if he would make good his threat. Would he go to the Immigration officials himself?

She punched the correct line and lifted the receiver. "Hello, Jeb. How are things with you?"

"Fair to middling, but I'm ready for a change of scene. I hate Washington in the summertime."

"Isn't it about time to wind things up there for this session?"

"It won't be long now. The House finally passed the tax package. It'll go before the Senate next week. Passage there looks fairly certain. They'll probably adjourn the week after next. Then my wife and I are going to rent an RV and wander around Canada for a month."

"Sounds wonderful."

"Yeah, I can't wait. Well, let's see here—I wanted to bring you up-to-date on a couple of things. First, the Gresham case. I just heard from our contact in Vietnam. The boy's grandparents agreed to accept Gresham's offer in exchange for the boy. In fact, they brought him with them to Ho Chi Minh City—Saigon—yesterday and turned him over to our man when the money changed hands. We didn't expect things to culminate so quickly. We thought they'd draw out the negotiations to get every dollar they could. I guess they figured a bird in the hand... Anyway, we didn't expect a decision for at least a couple of weeks. The contact said they acted like they just wanted to get rid of him."

"Where is Van now?"

"He spent the night at the Australian embassy. They're putting him on the next plane out. We'll get somebody in New York to meet his plane and put him on an Oklahoma City flight the day after tomorrow. I can't give you an ETA yet. When and if I can, I'll call you. It might be a good idea, though, if you'd tell Gresham to meet every flight coming in from Chicago on that day—the boy will probably have to change planes there."

"I hope he doesn't get lost. He'll be frightened and unsure. We don't even know if he can speak English."

"The flight attendants will be briefed on the situation. They'll look after him." Drewly talked for five minutes more about another matter before he rang off.

Kathleen dialed Quinn's office. He'd be so happy to hear the news that he might get over being angry with her. Although she couldn't bring herself to make the commitment he'd asked for, she didn't want hard feelings between them.

"This is Kathleen Kerns in Congressman Smythe's office. May I speak to Mr. Gresham?"

"Mr. Gresham is out of town."

"Do you know where I can reach him?"

"Not right now. He just left this morning. He'll be in Washington for a few days. He phoned me from the airport and said he'd let me know later where he'll be staying, but I haven't heard from him yet. I'm sorry."

"Yes, so am I." Quinn had evidently decided to make good his threat to go around Kathleen. He was going to feel pretty foolish when he learned that his trip had been unnecessary. Kathleen pondered her options. She wanted to give Quinn the news herself. She wanted to be sure he understood the scenario completely. Perhaps she just wanted to hear his voice. "Will you give him a message when he checks in?"

"Of course."

"Tell him..." Kathleen hesitated, wondering how to phrase it. She wasn't sure Quinn had told his secretary about his son. "Tell him the party he's expecting from Asia will be arriving in New York some time tomorrow."

"His son's on the way? How wonderful!"

Kathleen released a tense breath. Good. The secretary already knew about Van. "That's right. Tell him we've arranged for somebody to meet the New York flight and get Van on another to Oklahoma City. I'm sure Mr. Gresham will want to be here to meet him."

"You bet. He wouldn't miss it for anything."

Kathleen went home that evening, still thinking about Van's imminent arrival. At the back of her mind was a niggling fear that something would go wrong. Quinn and his secretary wouldn't make connections. Van would lose his way in the labyrinthian sprawl of the Chicago airport. Or his New York flight would be too late for him to reach Chicago before the second plane departed. She told herself there was no cause to worry. If Quinn didn't call his office, his secretary could meet Van's flight herself. The flight attendants would look after Van. Everything would work out.

Nevertheless, she was glad when Maggie phoned as soon as she got home.

"Got any plans for tonight?" Maggie asked.

"No, I was thinking about going to a movie or something."

"How about if I come over and we order a pizza? One of my favorite Hitchcock films is going to be on Channel 5 at eight."

"Come on over whenever you want."

"Seven, then."

"Good. That'll give me time to unwind." Kathleen decided to shower and put on a light cotton gown and robe, thankful that she'd have Maggie's company for the evening. Alone, she knew she'd keep worrying about Van. You're going to have to forget about that child, she lectured herself as she stepped into the shower. You aren't responsible for him, and you don't want to be. You can't afford to get involved. Isn't that why you sent Quinn away?

Maggie arrived. "Beware of lodgers carrying gifts," she said, handing Kathleen a foil-wrapped batch of chocolate chip cookies still warm from the oven.

Kathleen raised an eyebrow. "I consider myself warned. What have you been up to? Building fires on the carpet? Drawing crayon murals on the walls?"

Maggie laughed. "Nothing that bad. Let's order our pizza, and we'll talk."

They ordered the supreme, with everything on it, and sat at Kathleen's breakfast bar to eat the warm, cheese-dripping slices. "Umm," Maggie murmured around her first bite, "this is heavenly. I'd eat pizza five nights a week if it weren't so fattening." She swallowed and patted a rounded hip. "If you think I'm fat now, this is nothing to what I'd be if I didn't limit myself to one binge a week."

"You aren't fat."

"Okay, plump. Fortunately Bert likes a little plumpness."

"Speaking of Bert," Kathleen said with a twinkle in her eye, "I haven't seen him around lately."

Maggie reached for a glass of cola. "I asked him for time to think, and he gave it to me. No argument. No pressure."

"Wise man." Kathleen was sure Maggie's big secret had to do with Bert, but Maggie would get around to it in her own time.

"Yeah, I like that about him. He listens to what I say and assumes I know what I want. He called me last week just to ask how I was. He said he didn't want to be a pest, so he'd let me call him the next time I wanted to talk."

"Ah, he put the ball in your court."

Maggie nodded. "Right. At first I was kind of peeved. I was raised to accept the traditional roles for men and women. Bert's the man, so he's supposed to do the pursuing. When I was young, nice girls didn't phone boys." She chuckled. "After a day or two of that kind of thinking, I realized how silly I was being. Bert was only doing what I'd asked him to do. So I called him last night."

Here it comes, whatever it is, Kathleen thought. "And?"

"We talked for more than an hour. I may have to take out a loan to pay my phone bill, but it was worth it. We understand each other a lot better now. Bert's a wonderful man, Kathleen."

Kathleen got up to take the cola bottle from the refrigerator and refill their glasses. Grinning, she said, "I kind of guessed you felt that way."

"After we talked I wasn't scared anymore, and I was finally able to make some decisions I've needed to make."

Kathleen sat down and lifted her glass. "Scared? Surely not of Bert."

Frowning thoughtfully, Maggie plucked an olive from her pizza and popped it into her mouth. "Not of Bert. Of going too fast and making mistakes. Of taking chances and getting hurt, or making a fool of myself."

"And of being disloyal to Dink's memory?"

"A little," Maggie admitted. "But I got over that quickly, because I knew Dink wouldn't want it. When Dink got sick, he said to me, 'Maggie, however this turns out, I don't want you to stop living.' I knew he was telling me to marry again if I found somebody I could love. Of course, at the time, I didn't think I ever would."

"I take it Bert has mentioned marriage."

Maggie's smile was soft. "Last night. I told him I couldn't give him an answer yet. He said he could wait until I knew what I wanted. So..." She looked at Kathleen; her eyes held a mixture of excitement and regret. "I've made a decision."

Kathleen sensed what she would say next, and she understood Maggie's regret. They had become close friends. "Go on."

"When my lease on the duplex expires next month, I'll be moving to Topeka." She reached across the bar and took Kathleen's hand. "The worst part of it will be not seeing you very often. You're one of the best friends I ever had. I'll miss you, Kathleen."

Kathleen squeezed Maggie's hand in return. "I'll miss you, too. But life goes on, things change. We'll still be friends, even though we won't see each other so frequently."

"You know, last night, after I'd talked to Bert, I wondered why I'd stayed in Oklahoma City after Dink died. I did consider moving to Topeka at the time, but I didn't want to intrude on Ellen and Jeff's life. The real reason I stayed, though, was that this is where Dink and I lived the last five years of our marriage. We had friends here. I had a feeling that as long as I stayed where we'd been happy together, I could hang on to a little part of him. It was never the same, of course. Our friends began gradually dropping out of my life. It was nobody's fault. Their activities were geared to couples, and I didn't fit in anymore. Finally I decided to sell the house, but I still couldn't make the decision to leave the city. So I moved in here. This past year has been a sort of preparation stage for me. Now I'm ready to move on to the next stage."

Maggie took a bite of pizza and chewed it slowly. Then she went on, "I'm going to rent an apartment in Topeka. Nowhere near Ellen and Jeff. I don't want them to feel I'm camping on their doorstep."

"You know they wouldn't think that."

"We've got a great relationship, and I want to keep it that way. I'll be seeing a lot of Bert on his home ground. I can take my time and be sure of my feelings before I say yes to marriage.''

She hadn't mentioned the possibility of a negative answer, Kathleen noted. The oversight gave away more of Maggie's feelings than she'd even admitted to herself. ''Sounds like a sensible plan.''

''Well, I haven't told Ellen yet.''

''She'll be thrilled to have you so close. Sara, of course, will be ecstatic.''

Maggie grinned. ''I'm going to have to watch myself. I know I'll be tempted to drop in to see my granddaughter without waiting to be invited. But I won't do it.''

''You can always invite Sara to your apartment for a visit.''

''You're right,'' Maggie said. ''I'd already thought of that.'' She paused, sobering. ''I know just moving to where Bert lives is a pretty big step, but nothing worth having in life is ever gained without risks. I could stay here for the rest of my life, afraid to change anything because it might be a mistake, but what kind of life would that be?''

''Boring,'' said Kathleen.

Maggie nodded. ''I knew you'd understand. I'm sure you'll have no trouble finding another renter.''

''I know I won't.''

''Go ahead and advertise if you like. I'll be glad to show the place.''

''Okay. Thanks.'' Kathleen gazed into the pizza box. ''Want to split this last piece?''

"Sure."

Kathleen divided the triangle and handed Maggie half. "There's one thing I want understood, though."

Maggie's hand paused en route to her mouth. "What?"

"I want an invitation to the wedding."

Maggie blinked and then laughed. "If there's a wedding—"

"I'd bet money on it," Kathleen cut in.

"—you'll be one of the first to know."

They turned the lights low to add to the mysterious atmosphere and became thoroughly absorbed in the movie. Afterward they ate chocolate chip cookies with frosty glasses of milk.

Later Kathleen lay in bed and contemplated the changes that were about to take place in Maggie's life. Illogically, a part of her envied Maggie the adventure and challenge of it. She turned on her side, determined to fall asleep quickly. But she couldn't. She had succeeded in banishing Van from her thoughts while Maggie was there, but now the nagging worry returned. The changes Van was experiencing were far more chaotic than those Maggie was about to make. Was he still at the Australian embassy? Or already en route to New York? What was he thinking right now? Did he want to travel halfway around the globe to a father and a world he knew nothing of? He'd been given no choice in the matter. He was being bundled and shipped like a piece of furniture. The poor child probably didn't understand half of what was happening. He must be confused and frightened. Perhaps she would call Quinn's secretary tomorrow, just to make sure Quinn planned to be at the Oklahoma City airport to meet Van.

The phone call to Quinn's secretary the next day eased Kathleen's mind. Yes, Mr. Gresham had received the message and would be returning to Oklahoma City in time to meet his son's flight. Kathleen managed to get through the day without thinking about Van more than a half-dozen times.

She was watching television at home that evening when the local station broke into the network program with a weather advisory. Having lived in Oklahoma and Texas all her life, Kathleen was accustomed to storm watches and storm warnings. She knew what precautions to take when a tornado was sighted in the area, and otherwise she didn't worry overmuch about storms. But this bulletin concerned her. Much of the eastern third of the country was in for severe thunderstorms, with hail and high winds during the night. The forecaster described the front as the most severe of the season so far. If the storm continued to move in its present direction and at its present speed, Oklahomans could expect the worst of it in about twenty-four hours. Kathleen thought of Van on a plane flying through the turbulence, or making an unscheduled landing if continuing the flight became too dangerous. Either way he would be alone in a foreign country and terrified.

Updated weather reports interrupted the network programming several times during the next two hours, with little change in the original forecast. Kathleen found herself praying silently, Let that little boy be all right.

She was getting ready for bed when the telephone rang. "Kathleen...Kathleen, can you hear me?" There was so much static on the line that it was difficult to understand.

"Quinn?"

"Yes, I hope..." His voice faded away and came back. "...wake you."

"No, I wasn't asleep. Where are you?"

"Washington. They've canceled all flights because of the storm. I don't know when I'll be able to get out of here."

"But Van's on his way here, unless his flight is canceled, too."

"I know. That's why I'm calling. He's supposed to arrive at midnight. Could you possibly meet him and stay with him at my place until I get there? I don't know what shape he'll be in. There's nobody else I can trust to handle it."

A surge of static gave Kathleen a few moments to sort through her feelings. There was resentment at Quinn for putting her in the middle of a situation that she had promised herself not to become involved in. But whom else did he have to turn to? For all she knew his secretary was totally unable to handle the job.

Foremost in Kathleen's mind was concern for the boy. That concern easily won over the other feelings.

"Let me get something to write with. Now, give me the airline and flight number."

He had to repeat the information three times in order for her to hear it all over the static. "The front door key is hidden in the cedar planter to the left of the door. With this weather, the flight will probably be delayed or canceled. But somebody has to be there."

"I understand."

"Thanks, Kath. I didn't know what I was going to do if you refused."

"Try not to worry about Van. I'll be waiting for him."

"Kath..."

"Yes?"

"I shouldn't have come to Washington in the first place. I've been acting like a jackass."

"Don't think about that now."

"I'll apologize properly later. I'm going to stay at the airport until I can get a flight. You can have me paged if you need to talk to me. Try to make Van understand that I wanted to meet him."

"I will."

"Night, Kath."

"Good night."

It was already after eleven. The plane, if it arrived at all, would probably be late, but she wanted to be at the airport on time. There was always the possibility that Van's flight had taken off ahead of the storm. She dressed hurriedly in jeans and a knit shirt, stuffed a change of underwear and a nightgown into her large shoulder bag and made a quick, unsuccessful search for her umbrella. Finally she grabbed a raincoat, in case it started to rain before she got to Quinn's house, and ran to her car.

Grimacing, Kathleen emptied the bitter machine-dispensed coffee into a drinking fountain. She had arrived at Will Rogers International Airport two hours ago, drunk two previous cups of coffee and paced the silent, echoing terminal until her feet hurt. Because of the storm, the expected arrival time of Van's flight had already been put back three times. When she'd last asked, the flight was due to arrive at two-forty, fifteen minutes away.

She walked down the corridor to the rest room. She felt faintly nauseated from all the coffee she'd drunk. She washed her face with cold water and reapplied lip gloss. Then she went back to the airline counter.

"Any further word on Flight 602 from Chicago?"

"We still expect it at two-forty," the attendant said.

Kathleen thanked him and wandered to the plate glass wall overlooking the gate where the plane would unload its passengers. Because of the airport lighting, she couldn't tell if the sky was cloudy or clear. She hoped it wouldn't rain until she and Van were safely inside. She didn't know what kind of storms they had in Vietnam, but an Oklahoma thunderstorm could be frightening to the uninitiated. She would prefer not to have that particular fear added to an already shaky situation.

Several other people were in the waiting area now. They were all looking out at the night, as Kathleen was, anxious for a reassuring sight of their loved ones.

It was two-forty-three when they saw the plane slowly approaching the passenger bridge. A collective sigh of relief went through those who were waiting. Kathleen moved nearer the railing as the passengers began to straggle into the terminal. Only Kathleen and a young man were still waiting when a stewardess appeared in the corridor with a young boy. He was small for his age, by American standards, and painfully thin. His features were plainly oriental—hair black and straight, cheekbones flat and wide, nose small, eyes faintly slanted and as dark as midnight.

Kathleen approached. "Van Thieu?"

The stewardess smiled, but the boy's expression did not change. He appeared to be dazed from exhaustion. "I'm supposed to turn Van over to his father.

Kathleen extended her hand. "I'm Kathleen Kerns, a friend of Mr. Gresham. He was scheduled to return from Washington today, but his flight was canceled. He asked me to stand in for him."

"Well, here's your young man. We've been through a lot of turbulence. He was very brave, a wonderful passenger. This is Ms. Kerns, Van. She'll take good care of you."

"Hello, Van. Please call me Kathleen."

"How do you do?"

"You speak English. That's good."

"All the children in the orphanage are taught to speak English." He enunciated the words with care, his dark unblinking eyes studying her warily.

Kathleen started to take his hand, then decided he might resent her touching him. How did the Vietnamese feel about such familiarities? "Shall we go find your luggage?"

He took a baggage claim ticket from his shirt pocket and nodded. "Goodbye, Van," the stewardess said. "I hope you like your new home."

"This way," Kathleen said. He walked beside her stiffly, looking straight ahead. "You must be very tired. We're going to your father's house. It won't take long once we've found your things."

He seemed to hesitate for a moment, then said, "Yes, please." Which could mean almost anything. A frightened child, Kathleen thought, and much too lonely.

Van's worldly goods were contained in a single cardboard suitcase. Its lock was broken, and it had been tied with a rope to keep it closed. In the car Kathleen showed him how to buckle his seat belt. "Just like on the plane," she stated, and he nodded solemnly. Once they were on the freeway she said, "Everything will be strange to you at first, but you'll come to like it."

"America is a very big country."

She was encouraged by this unsolicited observation and sought to keep the conversation going. "Have you seen a map of the United States?"

"In the orphanage we see such a map."

"Well, Oklahoma—that's the name of the state we're in—is in the middle of the country. If I can find a map at your father's house I'll show you."

"Yes, please." He looked over at her hesitantly. "When will I see my father?"

"Just as soon as he can get on a plane. His flight was canceled because of the storm. He was very disappointed. He wanted so much to meet you himself. Did—did your grandparents talk to you about him?"

"No. They tell me only that I go to America and live with my father. I do not know why. Perhaps you will tell me."

He sounded so forlorn. Kathleen wanted to hug him, but again she feared a negative reaction. "Your father had to leave Vietnam when you were a baby. He—" Heavens, Quinn should be making these explanations. But Quinn wasn't here, and Van needed to be reassured. "He lost track of you because of the war, but he never stopped searching for you. As soon as he learned you were with your grandparents, he wanted to bring you here."

He turned to peer out the side window. Perhaps he was pondering what she'd said. It was impossible to tell. He didn't speak again during the drive. Kathleen turned on the radio and found some soft music. Although she'd never been inside Quinn's house, she was familiar with the affluent neighborhood, had, in fact, driven through it several times. The house was a low, wide-eaved, rambling ranch house. The yard was well lighted, the exterior stone and rough cedar. A circular driveway took them to the front door.

"Here we are," Kathleen said. She got out and retrieved Van's suitcase from the back seat. He hadn't moved. She opened his door. "Need some help getting out of that seat belt?"

"Yes, please."

She set the suitcase down and unbuckled him. He was staring at the house, his eyes wide. "This is my father's house?"

"This is it. Come on."

He climbed slowly. "He has many children?"

"No, dear. Only you."

He darted an amazed glance at her. "It is very large, very—" he searched for an adequate word "—expensive."

"Probably," Kathleen agreed. "He said the key was in this planter. Yes, here it is." She unlocked the door. "Are you coming?"

He followed her inside, his head swiveling back and forth, as he tried to look everywhere at once. "My father's parents and cousins live here perhaps. Do you know how many?"

"Your father lives here alone. Now you'll live here with him."

She turned on lights, found the room Quinn had described as Van's and put his suitcase on the bed.

When she returned to the living room he was still standing beside the door, as though he were afraid of going any farther.

"It must take much time to keep such a large house so clean," he said gravely. "Perhaps that is why my father sent for me."

The stoic assumption that his father could only want him to work for him—like Van's grandparents— brought tears to Kathleen's eyes. She went down on her knees and hugged him, forgetting to worry about how he might react. He held himself stiffly in her arms, and she heard air escaping his lungs in surprise. She gave him a final hug and sat back on her heels. "Your father sent for you because he wants you with him. Sons should be with their fathers."

His dark eyes regarded her, his thoughts veiled. Such adult circumspection and wariness unnerved her. She hoped Quinn wouldn't be delayed too long.

Chapter Thirteen

Are you hungry?'' Kathleen asked. Van had seated himself stiffly in a chair in the living room and hadn't budged. Kathleen was reminded of a small animal that takes on the coloring of his environment and becomes motionless to avoid detection.

"I eat on the airplane. Orange juice. Many peanuts." He rubbed his stomach and drew a deep breath.

Unaccustomed to such delicacies, he'd probably overdone it. "Are you feeling ill?"

"No," he said too quickly. "I am well. I do not cause trouble."

Kathleen stood in front of his chair, looking down at him. This small, frightened child would break her heart yet. He looked up at her, wary-eyed. "Being ill isn't causing trouble, Van. I can probably find something—some medicine—for an upset stomach. You must tell me how you feel."

He continued to stare at her for a long moment, measuring her. Maybe he thought her solicitousness was a trick. Kathleen shuddered to think of what he'd been through to make him so suspicious of others. "You tell me where this medicine is. I take it if I feel unwell."

He's not admitting to anything, Kathleen thought. She entered the bathroom from a hall that separated the living area of the house from the bedroom wing. The bathroom was large, with an oversize, sunken tub, separate stall shower and sauna. The fixtures and tile were in shades of brown, from the palest beige to dark chocolate. The wall next to the sauna was glass; the yard lights beyond the glass revealed a hedge-enclosed garden with a fountain and fishpond at its center. The bathroom was the most luxurious she'd ever seen. The entire house was, in fact, beautiful; several of the rooms were furnished with European antiques, probably pieces Quinn had picked up during his buying trips.

Sliding back a section of glass, she uncovered the medicine cabinet and found a bottle of antacid tablets. She showed the bottle to Van, who hadn't moved from his chair. "I'll set these on this table. If your stomach feels upset, you can chew one. They don't taste bad at all. Would you like one now?"

After a pause, he said, "Yes, please," and she handed him one. He chewed it slowly.

"Well, come along and I'll show you your room." Van's room was furnished with twin beds, a maple dresser and a desk. It looked like a boy's room; Quinn must have furnished it recently. It wasn't large or elaborate, particularly when compared with the rest of the house, but Van seemed overwhelmed by it. He stood uncertainly in the doorway while she tried to orient him. "I put your clothes in these drawers here. You can sleep in whichever bed you like." She smiled at him, but he didn't respond. She went on, "This door leads to your bathroom." She opened it. "The towels are here, if you'd like to take a bath before going to bed. It's very late, and I think we'd both better get some sleep now, don't you?"

"Where will you sleep?"

"Right next door. Just call if you need anything." She left him alone, not knowing what else to do. Perhaps once he was left to his own devices he'd explore the room and begin to feel more at ease. In the next room she put on her gown and robe and turned back the bedcovers. She listened for sounds from next door, but heard nothing. After a half hour she couldn't stand it any longer and went to Van's door. It was open. He'd changed into a pair of new cotton pajamas. Kathleen had noticed several sets of new underwear when she'd unpacked his things and wondered if somebody at the Australian embassy had purchased a few things for him. He must have come from his grandparents with practically nothing. Van was sitting on the side of one of the beds. He glanced up quickly when she appeared in the doorway, and she saw something like relief in his eyes. Had she frightened him by leaving him alone?

She turned back the bedclothes and plumped the pillow. "Everything all right?"

He nodded and climbed into bed where he lay looking up at her. She'd never known a child who could be so still. Impulsively she bent and kissed his forehead. "Good night, Van." She turned out the light and had reached her own door when she heard him call.

"Kathleen." His voice sounded thin and shaky.

She retraced her steps. "Yes?"

"I am sorry to cause trouble...."

Kathleen sighed. "Please stop saying that. You aren't causing trouble. Now, tell me what you want."

"I do not like the darkness."

Kathleen smiled. "Well, I can fix that. We'll leave the hall light on. How's that?"

"Thank you. In the house of my grandparents I like to burn a candle at night. They beat me if they discover it. Candles are expensive."

She went into the room and sat down on the unoccupied bed. "You can have as many lights here as you want, Van. Nobody will beat you."

He was silent for a bit. "You tell the lady from the airplane that you are my father's friend."

"That's right."

"You must know much about him. Will you tell me, please?"

Kathleen stretched out on top of the bedspread and turned on her side, her head resting in her hand. "What do you want to know?"

"What is his work?" '

"He's president of his own corporation. It's an importing firm. Hmm, how can I explain it to you?... He goes to other countries and buys pretty things. Like...oh, vases and tables, whatever he thinks Americans will buy. He brings them back here to America and they are sold in special stores—shops. Very costly stuff. I went into one of his stores once, but everything was too rich for my blood."

He frowned. "I do not understand this rich blood."

Kathleen laughed. "It's an expression. It means the merchandise was too expensive for me to buy."

"He has many people working in his shops?"

"I'm sure he does."

"Perhaps that is what he wants me to do. I will work in a shop. This I would not mind at all. It will be much better than working in the paddies."

Kathleen reached across the narrow space between the beds and took his small hand in hers. "Listen to me, pal. Children don't work in shops in this country. It's against the law."

His dark eyes pondered her. "This I do not understand. Why has my father brought me here?"

Had nothing she'd said sunk in? "To make a home for you. To take care of you. In the fall, two months from now, school will start. Your studies will keep you busy then. In the meantime I'm sure your father plans to spend as much time with you as he can. So the two of you can get acquainted."

Something she'd said had struck a chord. For a moment a spark of interest lit his eyes. "I enjoyed my studies at the orphanage. I like to read books. We had only three books in English, and I read them many times." He paused. "When my grandparents took me from the orphanage they said I did not need to study any longer. Farm workers have no need of books."

"Well, you won't be a farm worker here. You can study to be anything you want. A doctor. A teacher. Anything." He turned his head away and was silent for so long that she thought he'd fallen asleep. But when she started to release his hand, his fingers clutched hers. "Please, stay here with me."

"You know what I could do? I could sleep right here in this bed. Would you like that?"

His faint smile was answer enough. It was the first time she'd seen him smile.

"Do you think I could have my hand back?"

He nodded and released his grip. She got in between the sheets.

"Kathleen, why did my father wait such a long time to send for me?"

Kathleen felt helpless in the face of Van's too-adult skepticism. It seemed clear that he had never felt loved in his life; it might take quite a while for him to believe Quinn loved him. "He didn't know where you were, Van, or even if you were still alive. He hired men to find you, but none of them could until very recently. Believe me, as soon as they located you, he started the proceedings necessary to bring you to America." She was tempted to tell him that Quinn had paid his grandparents a great deal of money to get him. But knowing they'd exchanged him for money might serve more to hurt him than to convince him of Quinn's desire to have him.

"They said if I cause trouble, he will send me back." He was beginning to sound drowsy, his eyelids drooping.

"That's nonsense," Kathleen said emphatically. "Do me a favor, okay? Forget everything your grandparents told you about your father. Give yourself a chance to get to know him before you judge him. Will you do that?"

She wasn't sure he heard her. He didn't answer, and when she looked closer she saw that his eyes were closed. She lay back on her pillow. Tired as she was, it was some time before she fell asleep. She had just dozed off when she was awakened by sounds from Van's bed. He was crying in his sleep. She sat up, trying to shake the sleep from her brain.

"No, please!" Van whimpered. Then he mumbled something in Vietnamese.

Kathleen shook him gently. "Van, wake up, honey."

He cried, "No!" and struggled up from sleep.

"You're all right," she soothed. "You were having a bad dream."

He darted a glance about the room, as though to reassure himself of where he was. "He was whipping me," he said.

She stroked his forehead. "It was only a dream. Nobody is going to harm you. Can you go back to sleep?"

"You will not leave me?"

"No. I'll be right here."

That seemed to satisfy him. He turned on his side and was soon asleep. Whom had Van been dreaming about? she wondered. His grandparents? She blinked back tears of frustration. Van was a casualty of the Vietnam war, as surely as the soldiers who had been wounded on both sides. How many others like him were still over there in orphanages or on the streets? It was going to take a lot of love and patience to make him whole again.

Furthermore, she admitted, it was going to be the hardest thing she'd ever done to walk away from Van when Quinn got back.

After breakfast the next morning Kathleen took Van to the supermarket. She'd discovered that Quinn didn't keep a lot of food in the house. He probably ate out most of the time. But that would have to change now. Van needed a real home, with home-cooked meals on schedule. Quinn would just have to hire a live-in housekeeper. Kathleen hoped he could find a sweet, grandmotherly type.

Van was totally dazzled by the supermarket. He scurried up and down the aisles at Kathleen's heels, his eyes growing wider by the minute.

"I have never seen so much food," he said. "How can you decide what to buy?"

"I'm usually in a hurry when I grocery shop," Kathleen told him, "and I just grab whatever's easiest to fix. Today, though, we have plenty of time. What about these? Do you like raisins?"

"I do not know. I have never eaten them."

"It's time you did, then. And we must have some oranges and apples."

By the time they'd finished their basket was heaped to overflowing. As the groceries were being sacked, Kathleen lifted two big Delicious apples, polished them on her shirt and handed one to Van. "Washington apples," Kathleen said. "The best in the country."

Back at Quinn's house she put the groceries away and jotted down menus for their lunch and dinner. Van stayed at her heels, following her wherever she went in the house. When she went into the bathroom and shut the door, he waited for her in the hall outside. It finally dawned on her that he was afraid to let her out of his sight, afraid she would abandon him.

"Hey, I'm not going anywhere, pal," she told him. He listened, but trailed her back to the kitchen when she went to make a casserole for their lunch. They'd had a rain shower during the night, but the storm that had been predicted had veered to the north of Oklahoma City. The sky had cleared, and it looked as though it would be a warm summer day. In the sunlight that was falling through the kitchen windows she noticed that Van's cheeks seemed flushed. "Are you feeling all right, Van?"

He nodded emphatically. "Yes."

The phone rang as she was setting the casserole in the oven. It was Quinn.

"Kath, how's everything there?"

"We're managing. Van and I went to the supermarket this morning. We couldn't find much around here to eat. Are you still in Washington?"

"Yes, at the airport. I have a seat on a flight that's about to take off. I should be in Oklahoma City early this evening. My car's at the airport, so I'll be at the house about seven."

"Oh, good. You—" Kathleen smiled at Van, who was watching her closely. "You are definitely needed here. Would you like to speak to Van?"

"Yes, put him on."

"Van, your father wants to speak to you." She handed him the receiver. He listened, saying only "Yes, sir," a few times. When he hung up, he turned to Kathleen. "My father is coming home."

"I know. He'll be here in time to have dinner with us. Van?" He was still standing beside the phone, his head bowed. She went to him and put her arm around him. "You okay?" She brushed back the lock of black hair that had fallen across his forehead. "You're burning up! My goodness, you've got a fever. Why didn't you tell me you're sick? No, never mind. You don't want to cause any trouble, right? You're going to take some aspirin and go to bed, young man. You've had too much strange food. Too much excitement."

"You will not leave me?" The eyes that looked up at her were fearful.

"I'll stay right here, honey. I promise. I'll leave your bedroom door open so I can hear you if you call me."

Alone in Quinn's roomy, stainless steel and smoked glass kitchen, she ate a portion of the casserole for lunch. When Van awoke from a feverish sleep his temperature had gone down, and she carried a mug of chicken broth and crackers to him on a tray. He fell asleep again almost at once.

The combination of jet lag and the strain he'd been under had exhausted him. She hoped he could sleep until Quinn came home; perhaps then he'd feel up to meeting another stranger, his father.

Kathleen tidied up the kitchen and made a banana pudding for dinner. After that she could find nothing else to do. She roamed the big house, thinking thoughts that had been kept at bay earlier by the need to deal with Van.

It wasn't going to be a simple matter of leaving him in his father's care as soon as Quinn arrived. In less than twenty-four hours Van had come to depend on her being there. She couldn't just walk out in the hope that he'd instantly transfer that dependence to Quinn. The fact was that she didn't know how he'd react to

Quinn. Or to her defection. What if he decided that he'd been right all along—that he could trust no one? What if he wouldn't respond to Quinn? What if he went into a severe depression?

Van needed stability, somebody he could count on. Given enough time, Quinn could win him over. But Quinn couldn't stop working; there would be days, even weeks, when he would have to leave Van in the care of others. More strangers to confuse the child further. What that little boy needed more than anything was what had been taken from him when he was a year old: a mother who was there when he needed her.

A dozen times during the long afternoon Kathleen told herself that Van wasn't her responsibility, but she could never quite make herself believe it. She'd accepted a degree of responsibility when she agreed to meet him at the airport. She could almost see the disappointment and fear in his eyes when she told him she was leaving.

What was she going to do? she wondered again and again. Well, the first thing was to talk to Quinn. She couldn't think any further than that. For all she knew he didn't want her anymore. He'd admitted that he'd been wrong to go to Washington, but that didn't mean he'd forgiven her for throwing his declaration of love back in his face. What a complicated mess she'd made of things by trying to protect herself from potential pain. She'd wanted to be in control, to have an existence devoid of chance. But Maggie was right; any life worth living was riddled with risks.

She heard Quinn's key in the front door at seven-thirty. Van, in his pajamas, was sitting at the kitchen table, watching her get dinner ready; his fever had gone, but he was still weak. At the sound of the front door opening he shot Kathleen a panicky look.

"It's your father," Kathleen said reassuringly.

She took a breath to steady herself and went into the living room. Quinn was stacking his luggage against a chair. He looked rumpled and tired. He straightened, and her eyes locked with his; instantly her heart gave a wild leap of joy. Her first impulse was to fly across the room to him. Her second thought was of Van in the kitchen, and she hesitated. Quinn looked like a man near the end of his rope with frustration and fatigue. He also seemed deeply worried, obviously concerned about his son. What had she expected?

"Where is he?"

"In the kitchen."

He strode across the room. After a moment's hesitation she placed a hand on his arm. "Quinn, wait. Before you meet him, there are a couple of things you should know."

He halted and turned to look into her face. His eyes were intensely blue and fathomless. He seemed to shake off some errant thought as he dragged his hands through his hair. "Thank you for being here," he said wearily. "The Washington airport was a madhouse today. I thought I'd go crazy trying to get on a flight."

His eyes assessed her gravely; she had no idea what he was thinking. "What do you think I should know?"

"He's been ill—no, it doesn't seem to be anything serious. He ran a temperature earlier, but he's better now. It was probably just the strain of the trip. The other thing is—he's convinced you sent for him to use him as a sort of slave laborer."

"What?" he asked blankly.

"First he assumed you wanted him to keep the house clean. When I disabused him of that notion, he decided you wanted him to work in one of your stores. I told him you had nothing like that in mind, but I'm not sure I convinced him. He's—oh, Quinn, he keeps saying he doesn't want to cause any trouble. His grandparents told him that if he did, you'd send him back." She hadn't known tears were so close; she blinked to clear her misty vision.

"Damn them! I'd like to have five minutes alone with those two—just five minutes!" His head came up. "I'll set him straight about why he's here. Don't worry."

Kathleen hovered in the background as Quinn greeted his son. Quinn gathered the stiff little body against his chest for a moment, then sat down next to Van at the table. Van looked terrified. He kept glancing at Kathleen to reassure himself that she was still there.

In the awkward silence she said, "I'll put dinner on the table."

With her hands thus occupied, she listened as Quinn talked to his son. He asked if Van was feeling all right and was assured that Van was well and didn't wish to cause anyone any trouble. Kathleen glanced over her shoulder in time to catch Quinn's helpless look. Quinn went on to reiterate what Kathleen had already told Van, that his home was with Quinn now, that he would go to school in the fall and make new friends, that Quinn wanted him to be happy. Van listened silently; it was difficult to know whether he believed Quinn or not.

During dinner Quinn and Kathleen tried to keep a three-way conversation going, but Van's English vocabulary seemed to have shrunk to "Yes, please." Finally Kathleen sent him to wash his hands and brush his teeth in preparation for going to bed. He left the kitchen only after securing Kathleen's promise that she wouldn't leave while he was in the bathroom.

"He thinks I'm going to run out on him," she said when Van was gone.

"Perfectly understandable. Everybody else in his life has," Quinn said grimly.

"Last night he was so frightened of being left alone that I slept in his room. He's scared of the dark, too, so I left the hall light on. He's going to need a light every night for a while."

Quinn placed his elbows on the table and covered his face with his hands in a gesture of helplessness. "Could you possibly stay overnight again?"

"I was thinking that I should."

He lifted his head and smiled gratefully. "I can't seem to get through to him."

"Give it time, Quinn."

He reached out and placed his hand on her hair, an oddly gentle caress. "There's so much I want to say to you, Kath. I—"

"Kathleen?" Van was standing in the kitchen doorway.

Reluctantly Kathleen turned her gaze away from Quinn. "Ready for bed, pal?"

He nodded solemnly. Kathleen left the table and Quinn said, "Good night, son."

"Good night."

"I found a book of stories today," Kathleen said as she tucked Van into bed. "Would you like me to read to you until you fall asleep?"

"Oh, yes. I would like that very much."

Quinn can do this tomorrow night, Kathleen thought as she settled into a chair and opened the book. It will be a way for him to get closer to his son.

Chapter Fourteen

Kath, wake up."

Quinn's mouth was close to her ear, his warm breath stirring her hair. She'd fallen asleep in the chair beside Van's bed, the book still open in her hand. Straightening, she closed the book and laid it on the floor. Van was sleeping peacefully. She stretched her cramped back and squinted at Quinn. He wore a white terry robe, and still smelled of the soapy shower he'd taken.

He took her hand. "Come with me."

He led her from the room and down the hall to the huge master bedroom. He closed the bedroom door behind them and turned to face her.

"Quinn, if Van wakes up and I'm not there he'll be frightened."

He placed his hands on her upper arms and pulled her against him. His fingers bit convulsively into her skin. His mouth came down hard on hers. It was a kiss of desperation. His tongue forced its way between her lips to seek and possess, as if he would perish without the taste of her in his mouth.

When he pulled away he stared at her for a long, silent moment; then with a soft oath he released her. "He'll call if he wants you. We have to talk."

Although she was uncertain whether it was fear or joy, Kathleen trembled with emotion as he turned and walked a few steps away from her. For a moment he stood motionless, his head bowed, as though he were gathering his strength for some dreaded task.

She loved him with every fiber of her being. She had since she was a teenager, and she supposed she always would. When you cleared away all the accessory confusion in their relationship, everything came down to that one fact. She could feel her pulse throbbing in her ears as she glanced distractedly about her.

The room was elegant in a dignified, masculine style, with a corner fireplace of rough-hewn stone and a thick forest-green carpet. She drew a breath and darted a look at Quinn's back.

"Quinn..."

He turned around and crossed to her. His eyes locked with hers. "Sit down, Kath."

Slowly she lowered herself to the edge of the king-size bed. None too soon, she thought; her knees felt wobbly. "I—I've done a lot of thinking the past twenty-four hours...."

"No. I'll talk first." His hand came to rest on her shoulder, as though of its own accord; he gazed at her for a long moment, squeezed gently and pulled his hand away. With an abrupt shake of his head he crossed to a window, fiddled with the blind, uttered a curse and turned to face her. "I'm in over my head here, Kath. I have no idea how to handle an eleven-year-old child who's obviously been traumatized by God-knows-what cruelties."

"I know. You just have to take it one day at a time. He'll come around."

"I'm not so sure. You saw how he was with me. You've spent one day with him, and he already trusts you." Almost angrily, he strode to a small bar concealed in a massive antique chest. He poured a whiskey and drank. "I don't know. Maybe children have a natural instinct to trust women more than men."

"I think it's more complicated than that." She spread her hands on her knees. "I think the men in Van's life—particularly his grandfather—have been cold and demanding." She pressed a hand to her temple and shook her head. "He—he's probably never known a man who was kind to him."

He looked at her curiously. "What do you think it will do to him when you walk out of here? You can't lavish attention on him for a day or two, then go blithely on your way."

"No." She shook her head again, instinctively wanting to defend herself. "It will certainly not be blithely."

"Maybe you won't see it that way," he countered, "but he will." He crossed to stand before her. "Do you think it makes it all right because you lost your baby and you're afraid to love another child?''

"That's not fair, Quinn."

"Were you fair to me when you decided not to tell me about our daughter?''

"I wasn't thinking in those terms. I just wanted to—''

"Pretend it never happened." His voice was low and tense. "You cut the memory of Lauren out of your life, and me with it. You hurt me badly, Kath. You made me so angry I had to do something. Like an idiot, I went to Washington. I was going to storm my way into the office of the highest Immigration official I could find. I was going to demand that Van be sent to me. I felt like a fool when a secretary told me that Van was already on the way. I'm not sure what I was trying to prove. Maybe that I didn't need you. But that's a lie. I still want you to be my wife. I still need you, Kath. Now more than ever.''

"That night when you walked out on me—''

"I didn't walk out! You kicked me out.''

"I was trying to make you understand my feelings. You were talking about our being together. You didn't say anything about marriage.''

"I assumed that was understood.''

She shrugged helplessly. "I wasn't assuming anything. At any rate, I've thought of little else today. That's what I've been trying to say to you. If you still want me.... Van needs a mother, Quinn. Too many people have let him down. I can't be another one.''

He watched as she gripped the side of the bed. "I see. And if you hadn't picked Van up, spent some time with him, would you be saying this? If Van weren't here, would you trust me enough to risk marrying me?''

"I don't know." Her eyes darkened with confusion. "It might have taken longer for me to come to terms with it."

Quinn drank more Scotch. "Damn it, Kathleen." He walked back to the bar and filled his glass again. "You're not making it easy to say what I have to say," he managed in a calmer tone, his back to her. "God knows I'll take you on almost any terms, but my ego's taking a beating." He ran a tense hand through his hair. He looked back at her, his eyes intense. "You're the only woman in the world who can hurt me and keep me coming back for more."

"Quinn." Kathleen shut her eyes and swallowed convulsively. "I'm sorry. When I was seventeen I loved you—worshiped you. I wanted to die when I heard you were missing. I wanted it even more when Lauren died. I didn't know any other way to deal with all the grief except to deny it, block it from my mind. To do that I had to block out my love for you."

"Yes. I understand that now. I was too angry for a while to do anything but act like a fool." His tone was flat. "While I was in Washington I finally understood." Kathleen opened her eyes and started to speak, but he held up a hand to stop her. He downed the last of his drink and set the glass aside. "Let me finish. I don't want you to say anything you'll want to retract after you've heard this. I've wanted to tell you several times during the past couple of months, but on reflection it always seemed better to wait."

He hesitated, then pulled a chair over from a corner and placed it facing Kathleen. He sat down, leaving several feet between them, as though he didn't want to be tempted to touch her. He spread his long fingers on the arms of the chair. "In hindsight, I'm not sure I did the right thing in keeping this from you."

The confusion in her expression deepened. "Quinn, what are you talking about?"

"Ask all the questions you want when I've finished," he said curtly. "But let me say this without interruptions."

Kathleen struggled for control. "All right. Say it."

"After I escaped from the Vietcong I stayed in a military hospital for ten days while they ran tests and built me up. As soon as they released me, I went to Saigon. I had the option of coming back to the States at that point, but I'd heard Patrick was in Vietnam, and I went back to find him. He'd changed, Kath. The war did something to him, killed something in him. You could see it in his eyes, and in the way he had always to be moving and doing. He couldn't relax; he couldn't sleep. There were times when I thought he was going to come apart." His fingers clenched on the arms of the chair, then slowly relaxed. "He needed to get out of there. I tried to get him to see a doctor, but he wouldn't. I told him that I was thinking of going to his commanding officer and reporting his mental condition. He said he'd kill me if I did that."

Kathleen's throat ached. "Quinn, you know he couldn't have done that."

He studied her for a moment. "The old Patrick couldn't have, but the Patrick I knew in Vietnam might have. Anyway, it became a moot point, because he finally told me why he couldn't leave. He introduced me to his lover. They'd been together a few months. She was pregnant, and Patrick didn't know what to do about it. She'd lost her job, and her family had disowned her. She wouldn't have an abortion, and I gathered that Patrick couldn't bring himself to marry her and bring her to the States."

He'd told her not to ask questions, but she couldn't stop herself. "Didn't he love her?"

He let out a long breath. "I don't know. But he felt responsible for her. He *was* responsible; he was the father of her child. So he kept on the move to keep from thinking about it. He volunteered for the most dangerous duties; he was flying search-and-destroy missions back to back, twenty or thirty hours at a stretch. He made me promise to look after her if anything happened to him. Since he was courting death, I guess we both knew it was just a matter of time until he ran out of luck. Eventually he didn't come back from one of those flights." He looked away. "And he didn't have to decide what to do about Mai. His problems were over, and I was left to deal with them."

Kathleen stared at him. "Mai? You said Mai...."

His eyes shot back to hers again. "Yes, Mai was Patrick's lover. She loved him, and she wanted his child. Van is that child, Kath."

Kathleen clenched her hands together to keep them from shaking. "But you married her."

"It was the only way I could help her. Once she was my wife, she was eligible to receive a government allotment. The money provided food and shelter for her and Van. Without it she'd have ended up selling herself on the street to support her baby."

Kathleen was too stunned to feel much of anything. "Did you love her?"

Quinn said thoughtfully, "Yes, I loved her. Like a sister. She was a good woman who was caught in events over which she had no control. After Patrick was killed she had no one to turn to but me. We talked it over, and marriage seemed the only solution. As soon as I could get clearance for her, I planned to bring her to the States and help her make a life for herself and Van. Once she could stand on her own feet, we were going to get a divorce."

Tears blinded Kathleen's eyes. Quinn reached for her, but she pulled away. "It was a marriage of convenience, Kath. Mai and I never had . . . never made love."

"Why didn't you tell me this before?" She turned her teary face toward him. She shook her head when he reached out for her again. "You say I had no right to keep Lauren's existence from you. Well, you had no right to keep this from me. Why, Quinn? Why didn't you at least tell me when you came to my office for help in getting Van out of Vietnam?"

"During the years when I didn't know whether Mai was alive or dead I wasn't free to contact you. I still loved you, Kath. How could I come to you and tell you I was married to somebody else? Even if she was my wife in name only."

"When you came to my office, you knew she was dead."

"But you work for the congressman, and I needed the congressman's help to get Van out. I wasn't sure I'd be allowed to have Van if it was known that he wasn't really my son. I didn't want to put you in the position of having to lie to your boss and the Immigration officials."

Kathleen moistened her lips, her gaze intent on his face. "You know I would have done it without a qualm. Van is my brother's son. If you'd told me this the other night, when you were trying to convince me we could have a life together..." She said the last words with a dawning realization in her tone.

A quick flash of anger shot into his eyes. "Damn it, there's another reason I didn't tell you. I wanted you to come to me because you loved me, not because I had custody of Patrick's son. Believe me, I came close to telling you when you said that we might be able to make it together if Van didn't exist—but if I had, Van would still have been the main factor in your decision. It would have been emotional blackmail. But more than that, I wanted you to want to be with me, regardless of anything else." He waited a moment, watching her expression as she digested what he'd said. "Now you've agreed to marry me, after all, but more because of Van's needs than mine. Well..." He released a weary breath. "As I said earlier, I'll take you on any terms."

Kathleen stared at him for a long moment. She felt her muscles relaxing. "I haven't made my feelings clear," she said softly. "I should have."

Slowly she rose, and he came to his feet. In his expression the beginning of hope warred with caution. She loved every detail of his face; the suntanned skin; the light-colored brows, drawn together now in thought; the blue eyes, direct and expressive; the hard, masculine angularity of cheekbone and jaw. In that moment she knew that the love she had felt for him as a girl was but a feeble shadow of her woman's love. She could throw her whole heart and soul into loving him now.

"I love you, Quinn. There's never been a doubt in my mind about that. But I had the stupid notion that love always ends in pain, and that I couldn't risk it again. Now I know I'll risk anything to be with you." She lifted her hand to his brow as if to smooth away the tense furrows.

Then they reached out for each other, and they were locked in a fierce embrace, body hard against body, mouth seeking mouth. Her fingers buried themselves in his hair, still damp from the shower, and it came to her that she had come home at long last. In Quinn's arms she felt whole, as she never had when she was apart from him.

The words he murmured against her mouth were words that all lovers say, but to her they were unique and precious. Then there were no more words as his fingers fumbled with her clothing and he undressed her. He dropped the terry robe and they moved together, heated flesh against heated flesh. They communicated with tongues and lips and fingers with more expression and intimacy than mere words allowed.

He framed her face with his hands and vowed, "I mean to become so necessary to your happiness that you can't live without me."

She smiled. "You already are."

With breathless eagerness he pulled her down with him on the bed. Kathleen could feel the need shuddering through him with a desperation that matched her own. Their mouths and hands were rapacious, taking and giving. Their flesh, damp with perspiration, quivered under the sensual siege.

"Oh, Kath," Quinn gasped, "how I missed you. I'm nothing without you."

She ran restless, greedy hands over his back and lean hips. "I know," she moaned. "It's the same for me."

Fueled by the need racing through them, their passion exploded. She arched her body toward him, and he moved over her as frantic desperation overcame all else.

The pleasure of their joining bolted through her like lightning, rocking her as they moved together, faster and higher, reaching for the stars. Wave after wave of sensation washed over her, forcing the breath from her body in urgent, incoherent moans. The culmination came, racking them simultaneously. They floated from the height of ecstasy into the sweet, lulling pool of contentment.

They lay together in a silence that was somehow an intimate communion. She could feel his breath caressing her cheek. She turned her head and let her lips brush his.

"Quinn," she murmured, "you belong to me."

"That's right," he muttered drowsily. "You couldn't get rid of me if you tried."

Silence reigned for several minutes as she slid her hand lightly over his damp skin, reveling in her satisfaction.

"While we were doing all that talking," he said finally, his voice low and sleepy, "I meant to talk about the wedding."

"We got sidetracked."

He laughed softly, and his hand closed possessively over her breast. "Yeah, we did, didn't we?"

"Mmm." She kissed his chin and snuggled against him.

"I think we should get married as soon as we can get the license and blood tests. I want you here with Van and me. I want us to be a family. Does that sound all right to you?"

She ran her hand down his back. "It sounds wonderful. Quinn... will you tell Van about his real father?"

"Maybe. But not until he feels secure with us and he's old enough to understand. We'll take it a day at a time, as you said." He was silent for a moment, then he went on, "About the honeymoon... I don't see how we can leave Van right away."

"Of course we can't. We'll take him with us."

"Are you sure?" he murmured as his fingertips sought her nipple.

"Uh-huh." She shivered as his palm slid gently over the hardening tip. "Jeb Drewly and his wife are renting an RV this summer. We could do that. We could show Van a lot of his new country before school starts.''

"Hmm, I like that idea. But I insist on a private bedroom for you and me. I plan to ravish you at least twice a day.''

She smiled. "Van may get an education in more than geography.''

He lifted his head to kiss her. "He'll know that his parents love each other.''

"You're going to be a wonderful father, Quinn...." She meant to say more, but she lost her train of thought as his mouth found her throat. The last coherent thing she said for a long while was, "And a wonderful husband.''

OFFICIAL SWEEPSTAKES INFORMATION

1. **NO PURCHASE NECESSARY**. To enter, complete the official entry/order form. Be sure to indicate whether or not you wish to take advantage of our subscription offer.

2. Entry blanks have been pre-selected for the prizes offered. Your response will be checked to see if you are a winner. In the event that these are not claimed, a random drawing will be held from all entries received to award not less than $150,000 in prizes. This is in addition to any free, surprise or mystery gifts which might be offered. Versions of this sweepstakes with different prizes will appear in Torstar Ltd. mailings and their affiliates. Winners selected will receive the prize offered in their sweepstakes insert.

3. This promotion is being conducted under the supervision of Marden-Kane, an independent judging organization. By entering the sweepstakes, each entrant accepts and agrees to be bound by these rules and the decisions of the judges which shall be final and binding. Odds of winning in the random drawing are dependent upon the total number of entries received. Taxes, if any, are the sole responsibility of the prize winners. Prizes are non-transferable. All entries must be received by August 31, 1986.

4. This sweepstakes package offers:

1, Grand Prize	: Cruise around the world on the QEII	$100,000 total value
4, First Prizes	: Set of matching pearl necklace and earrings	$20,000 total value
10, Second Prizes	: Romantic Weekend in Bermuda	$15,000 total value
25, Third Prizes	: Designer Luggage	$10,000 total value
200, Fourth Prizes	: $25 Gift Certificate	$5,000 total value
		$150,000

   Winners may elect to receive the cash equivalent for the prizes offered.

5. This offer is open to residents of the U.S. and Canada, 18 years and older, except employees of Torstar Ltd., its affiliates, subsidiaries, Marden-Kane and all other agencies and persons connected with conducting this sweepstakes. All Federal, State and local laws apply. Void in the province of Quebec and wherever prohibited or restricted by law. Winners will be notified by mail and may be required to execute an affidavit of eligibility and release which must be returned within 14 days after notification. Canadian winners will be required to answer a skill testing question. Winners consent to the use of their names, photograph and/or likeness for advertising and publicity purposes in conjunction with this and similar promotions without additional compensation. One prize per family or household.

6. For a list of our most current prize winners, send a stamped, self-addressed envelope to: WINNERS LIST, c/o Marden-Kane, P.O. Box 10404, Long Island City, New York 11101.

SSR-A-1

Silhouette Special Edition

COMING NEXT MONTH

NOBODY'S FOOL—Renee Roszel
Cara never minded a little fun and games . . . but only on her own terms. So when businessman Martin Dante challenged her to a nine-mile race, she feared the results would be "winner take all!"

THE SECURITY MAN—Dixie Browning
Though Valentine had survived both a bad marriage and an accident that had left her widowed, she wasn't quite ready for her new handsome neighbor. Val couldn't risk loving, but with Cody it was all too tempting.

YESTERDAY'S LIES—Lisa Jackson
Iron willed and proud, Tory was not about to be manipulated, especially not by Trask McFadden. The attractive young senator had deceived her in the past—could he convince her that this time his love was real?

AFTER DARK—Elaine Camp
Sebastian was a man haunted by the past. Everly was a woman determined to control her future. Now he was back to reclaim her heart. Could she be convinced of the healing power of love?

MAGIC SEASON—Anne Lacey
Independence was her trademark and Game Warden Laura Marchand kept her image with spit and polish. But sportsman Ryan D'Arco was hunting her territory and was about to capture her heart.

LESSONS LEARNED—Nora Roberts
Juliet could smell success when she was assigned to do the publicity tour for Italy's most famous chef. But Carlo distracted her with his charms, setting his romantic recipes simmering in her heart.

AVAILABLE NOW:

Silhouette Special Edition

AMERICAN TRIBUTE

AMERICAN TRIBUTE

*American Tribute titles
now available:*

RIGHT BEHIND THE RAIN
Elaine Camp #301–April 1986
The difficulty of coping with her brother's
death brought reporter Raleigh Torrence
to the office of Evan Younger, a police
psychologist. He helped her to deal with
her feelings and emotions, including love.

THIS LONG WINTER PAST
Jeanne Stephens #295–March 1986
Detective Cody Wakefield checked out
Assistant District Attorney Liann McDowell,
but only in his leisure time. For it was the
danger of Cody's job that caused Liann to
shy away.

LOVE'S HAUNTING REFRAIN
Ada Steward #289–February 1986
For thirty years a deep dark secret kept them
apart—King Stockton made his millions while
his wife, Amelia, held everything together.
Now could they tell their secret, could they
admit their love?

Take 4 Silhouette
Special Edition novels
FREE
and preview future books in your home for 15 days!

When you take advantage of this offer, you get 4 Silhouette Special Edition® novels FREE and without obligation. Then you'll also have the opportunity to preview 6 brand-new books —delivered right to your door for a FREE 15-day examination period—as soon as they are published.

When you decide to keep them, you pay just $1.95 each ($2.50 each in Canada) *with no shipping, handling, or other charges of any kind!*

Romance *is* alive, well and flourishing in the moving love stories of Silhouette Special Edition novels. They'll awaken your desires, enliven your senses, and leave you tingling all over with excitement...and the first 4 novels are yours to keep. You can cancel at any time.

As an added bonus, you'll also receive a FREE subscription to the Silhouette Books Newsletter as long as you remain a member. Each issue is filled with news on upcoming books, interviews with your favorite authors, even their favorite recipes.

To get your 4 FREE books, fill out and mail the coupon today!

Silhouette Special Edition®

Silhouette Books, 120 Brighton Rd., P.O. Box 5084, Clifton, NJ 07015-5084